DISNEY · SQUARE ENIX

KINGDOM HEARTS

[chi]

THE NOVEL

Your Keyblade, Your Story

Tomoco Kanemaki

Original Concept
Tetsuya Nomura
Masaru Oka

Illustration by
Shiro Amano

NEW YORK

KINGDOM HEARTS χ: THE NOVEL
TOMOCO KANEMAKI,
ILLUSTRATIONS: SHIRO AMANO,
ORIGINAL CONCEPT: TETSUYA NOMURA, MASARU OKA

Translation by Luke Baker
Cover art by Shiro Amano

Yen On
150 West 30th Street, 19th Floor
New York, NY 10001

Visit us at yenpress.com
facebook.com/yenpress
twitter.com/yenpress
yenpress.tumblr.com
instagram.com/yenpress

First Yen On Edition: December 2019

Yen On is an imprint of Yen Press, LLC.
The Yen On name and logo are trademarks of Yen Press, LLC.

The publisher is not responsible for websites (or their content) that are not owned by the publisher.

Library of Congress Cataloging-in-Publication Data
Names: Kanemaki, Tomoko, 1975- author. | Amano, Shiro, illustrator. | Baker, Luke, translator.
Title: Kingdom hearts X : the novel / by Tomoco Kanemaki ; illustration by Shiro Amano ; translation by Luke Baker ; cover art by Shiro Amano.
Description: First Yen On edition. | New York, New York : Yen On, 2019. | "Original concept: Tetsuya Nomura, Masaru Oka"
Identifiers: LCCN 2019036787 | ISBN 9781975387341 (paperback) | ISBN 9781975387358 (ebook)
Subjects: CYAC: Fantasy. | Prophecies—Fiction. | Adventure and adventurers—Fiction.
Classification: LCC PZ7.1.K256 Kr 2019 | DDC [Fic]—dc23
LC record available at https://lccn.loc.gov/2019036787

ISBNs: 978-1-9753-8734-1 (paperback)
978-1-9753-8735-8 (ebook)

1 3 5 7 9 10 8 6 4 2

LSC-C

Printed in the United States of America

CONTENTS

Chirithy

Familiars known as "Spirits," which accompany each Keyblade wielder. They resemble gray cats with black stripes.

You

A Keyblade wielder assigned to Anguis, the Union under the leadership of Invi. You seek the truth of the worlds alongside Skuld and Ephemer.

Ephemer

A young Keybearer. Though he is a member of Unicornis Union, Ephemer often acts independently and breaks off from the group in search of answers to his questions.

Skuld

A girl with long black hair who wields a Keyblade. She is Ephemer's friend, and she later works alongside you, too.

The Master of Masters and the Six Apprentices

The Master of Masters

A mysterious man in a black coat who has six apprentices. He possesses the ability to see the future, and those visions are recorded in the Book of Prophecies. Creator of Chirithy.

Ava

One of the Foretellers. A young woman who wears a fox mask and is in charge of Vulpes Union. She is also the leader of the Dandelions.

Ira

A solemn young man in a unicorn mask who heads the Unicornis Union. Acts as leader of the five Foretellers.

Aced

One of the five Foretellers, he wears a bear mask. A dauntless Keyblade wielder and leader of Ursus Union. Ira's right-hand man.

Gula

A Foreteller in a leopard mask. Commands the Leopardus Union. A calm and collected youth who gets along well with Ava.

Invi

A female Foreteller in a snake mask who heads the Anguis Union. She strives to take an even-minded view of matters.

Luxu

The sole pupil of the Master of Masters who has never led a Union. Much like his teacher, he cloaks himself in black.

The world was pure darkness.

But I was born into a radiant world enveloped in a brilliant light.

From within that light, my master gazed upon me and smiled.

Mm, I'm so sleepy. I can barely keep my eyes open... Maybe I can catch a few more z's...

"Master, did you make this? It's so cute!" said a girl I didn't know. *She's wearing a fox mask—who's she? And...hmm. The man in the black coat must be my master.*

"Well, things are gonna get pretty hectic around here soon, but this Spirit Chirithy is gonna make your lives much easier. Hopefully," he said.

Oh, so that's my name. Chirithy. And I'm...some kind of creature. I kinda look like a gray cat with lots of black stripes.

"Spirit?"

That's right; I'm a Spirit. And now there's a boy with a mask like a leopard staring at me.

"You could say they're like...cats or dogs. And they'll be your loyal pets. Every wielder will have one of these adorable little guys at their side. They're here to help, so play nice."

"Okay!" replied fox-mask girl.

So there's going to be more of me... But how? No sense fretting about it, I guess. I'm still so sleepy, after all.

Long, long ago, all the worlds were still one. One day, this would be called the age of fairy tales. It all began here in Daybreak Town.

The Master of Masters had an eye that gazes into the future. He bestowed upon five of his six apprentices a copy of the Book of Prophecies, in which was written the events to come.

The reliable Ira, who wore the mask of the unicorn, was given his role to take over for the Master and to lead the others.

Similarly, the virtuous Invi, who wore the mask of the snake, was given her role to watch over the others with a fair eye.

The fearless Aced, who wore the mask of the bear, was given his role to support their brand-new leader, Ira.

The prudent Ava, who wore the mask of the fox, was given her role to prepare exceptional Keyblade wielders for the world after.

The coolheaded Gula, who wore the mask of the leopard, was given his role to uncover the mystery of the Book of Prophecies.

All five of them were entrusted with their own copy of the Book.

Luxu, the first of the apprentices to be given his role, watched his companions from afar, as they learned what it was that they were meant to do, then he disappeared.

Not long after that, the Master vanished, dimmed, faded without a trace.

This is where your story began—the story of your very own adventure.

Chapter 1

WHAT KIND OF POWER FLOWS WITHIN YOUR HEART?

Your story will now begin.

The heart that guides you… What form does it take?

When the light enfolded you, you awakened and took your first step.

You found yourself in Daybreak Town, in the familiar Fountain Square. But then darkness appeared, swelling and growing into an enormous humanoid form—the Heartless known as Darkside. The Heartless were manifestations of the heart's darkness that seek to take away the hearts of others—but how could you defend yourself?

Suddenly, a Keyblade appeared in your hand.

Your Keyblade held the power of light, the strength to drive back the darkness. You charged ahead as if you had known all along what you were going to do. You swung your Keyblade at Darkside, but you were batted easily aside and tumbled across the stones.

But as the Darkside reached for you, someone else arrived, Keyblade in hand, and knocked away the Heartless's arm.

Your rescuer was the Foreteller Invi, wearing a white robe and a serpent's mask. She lashed out with her Keyblade and drove the Heartless back into the darkness it had come from, then jumped in after it.

I guess we all have to start somewhere?

Anyway, that was when you were joined by your faithful companion Chirithy—in other words, me.

"Pretty scary stuff, huh? But you get an A for effort," I said to you.

You were still sitting on the ground, and you just blinked at me in surprise.

"You look a little confused. Here's what's going on." I came over beside you and cleared my throat. "Your pursuit of light made you the perfect candidate for a Keyblade wielder. Darkness is spreading, and it's up to you to use the weapon to get rid of it, collect light, and in turn save the world."

You just stared blankly back at me—guess that was a pretty dramatic place to start.

"I know it's a lot—are you still with me? The monster that was just defeated belongs to the darkness and is called a Heartless. These Heartless scour the world searching for hearts, spreading darkness as they go. The Keyblade is an effective weapon against them."

That didn't seem to do anything for your confusion, and I was starting to get a little worried. I leaned in closer.

"I hope this is all sinking in… Anyway, I was assigned by a certain someone to watch over a new Keyblade wielder—you! I'm Chirithy. I'll be supporting you the whole way, teaching you everything you need to know and more."

I extended a paw, and you took it.

"Nice to meet ya! Right now, that Keyblade is just like you—it has room to grow, and you'll need to learn to draw out its power. I know this is a lot to take in, so we'll pick this up again in a bit, okay?"

After I helped you get to your feet, you finally smiled.

That was good enough for me. "See you next time!" I called, then vanished with a somersault in the air. I think it startled you a little.

As you watched me go, others wielding Keyblades much like yours gathered around you, and shortly after that, the Foreteller Invi returned after driving off the Darkside.

"You've managed to tap into the power of the Keyblade," she told you quietly. "Lesser Heartless won't stand a chance, but in order to defeat stronger foes…you must combine your strength with those who share your purpose and aspirations. Your friends will become your power." She was referring to the Keyblade wielders around you.

Each Foreteller led one of the five Unions of Keyblade wielders, and the one you had chosen was Anguis. These five leaders all had a copy of the Book of Prophecies and a role given to them by their own leader, the Master of Masters, and they had formed these Unions according to his teachings. The Unions brought together Keyblade wielders like you to collect light in the form of Lux by defeating Heartless, creatures of darkness.

"There are others who collect the light, but not all of them share the same goal of bringing peace to the world. You must discover who amongst us walks the path of darkness."

With a somewhat disconcerting bit of advice, Master Invi took her leave, and the group of Keyblade wielders began to disperse.

What was this feeling stirring your chest? Hope? Anxiety?

Or maybe—something else.

"What happened? Are you okay?" I appeared before you again and watched you closely, trying to see what was going on inside your heart. "I know this is overwhelming, but darkness waits for no one! In fact, it's found its way to a bunch of other worlds, which need your help. I know a way to these places," I said, leading you to a brightly glimmering gateway.

Okay, time for your adventure to begin. Next stop, Dwarf Woodlands!

Your eyes filled with wonder as you took in this brand-new world.

You were in the midst of a dense forest, and every so often you could hear the twittering of little birds nearby.

"Uh-oh, we have a problem. A great light is about to be enveloped by darkness! Someone needs your help."

You nodded, and we headed deeper into the dimly lit forest. Heartless came after us along the way, but you made short work of them. Not bad at all for a beginner!

"Aha! Over there! The Heartless are attacking her," I shouted as I spotted a girl deep within the trees. She had black hair and red lips, and her dress was red and blue.

She was also surrounded by large, round Heartless the color of darkest night, and you ran toward her as fast as you could.

You brought your Keyblade down on one of the creatures, and it clawed back at you with one of its spindly arms. And yet you didn't falter. You only met it with a steely gaze before you switched over to magic to finish it off.

The girl was trembling, hunkered down with her eyes closed.

Once you made sure she was safely behind you, you sprang into the midst of the remaining Heartless. After dealing with them, you said something to the girl.

"Oh dear. Oh dear," she murmured. "I'm so afraid! It's much too dark and scary in this glade."

But when she finally opened her eyes, you smiled and raised your Keyblade, sending light over the both of you.

"Oh, you seem so warm and made of light. Was that your heart? Tell me, please."

Instead of answering, you just lowered your Keyblade and tilted your head in confusion.

"Yes, I'm sure it was! How sweet. Meeting you is quite a treat. Oh, how silly. I haven't introduced myself. My name is Snow White," the girl said with a cheerful smile. Snow White was someone very special.

Just then, you heard the eerie sound of flapping wings from deeper within the woods. Snow White looked up in surprise.

"I mustn't stay. It's too dangerous for me here. Good-bye!" She hurried off.

"That's her all right," I said, next to you. "She's a precious light, one the world can't afford to lose. That's why you need to watch over her."

You nodded to say you would, then hurried off after Snow White. After pushing your way through the thick underbrush, you found her surrounded by Heartless yet again.

Snow White's expression turned to relief when she saw that you had come to the rescue. "Oh, thank you! This forest is so scary when I'm alone."

You offered to lead the frightened girl out of the forest.

"Would you be so kind? I'd feel so much better if you would," Snow White said as she calmed down again.

You made your way through the trees with the girl in tow, but the deep, dark woodland seemed to go on forever. At long last, you came across a small cottage.

"Look! A cottage! Oh, thank you. I don't think I could have gotten here on my own."

You bobbed your head in acknowledgment. This little dwelling appeared to be under the protection of some mysterious power.

"Oh, it's adorable! Just like a doll's house." Snow White stepped inside, and you followed.

Tidy was not the word to describe the state it was in. There were dishes of half-eaten food scattered atop the wooden table, and clothes were strewn all over the floor, as if whoever had worn them had just taken them off and left them there.

Snow White let out a long yawn, sank down onto a diminutive bed, and promptly began snoring softly. Running from all those Heartless in the forest must have been exhausting.

"I can't think of a safer place for her to be," I commented.

You replied with a nod.

In one of the rooms of the clocktower overlooking Daybreak Town, Invi stood before the Master of Masters.

This was shortly before the Master disappeared.

Both of their faces were hidden; his beneath the hood of his long black coat, and hers behind her snake mask and white hood embroidered with gold thread and tied in the center with a blue ribbon.

"So, to sum it up, I'll need you to observe the others. Easy breezy," the Master informed her cheerfully.

"A-all right."

Though her mask obscured her expression, Invi's reply made her discomfort obvious.

Oddly enough, the Master seemed pleased by this reaction. "Like I said, Ira may have to take over for me... But don't be shy. Just be fair. And do not be afraid to speak up! Even though I say 'observe,' you'll need to be the mediator; make sure people get along," he explained lightly.

Invi's head was still lowered. "I understand, but...without you or Luxu, to form and maintain our own unions is..." She finally looked up. "It's a little unnerving, to be honest."

The Master walked up to her slowly. "Oh, come on. Lighten up a little! Maybe I'll never disappear." He peered into his apprentice's face. "Wait. Do you *want* me to go?"

Flustered, Invi shook her head vehemently. "What? N-no! Of course not!"

The Master chuckled. "I was just kidding!"

"I see...," she murmured, hanging her head again

"Look, I get that change can be hard for everyone," the Master of Masters told her. "But things need to keep moving forward." His head turned just the tiniest bit, as if he was looking away. "And you need to keep up. Otherwise, you'll just get left behind all alone. Now that you know what the future holds, Invi, what does your heart say?"

Invi raised her head. The Master didn't usually talk like this—something was slightly different.

"'May your heart be your guiding key,'" the Master continued. "I say it all the time; you ultimately need to do what your heart feels is right."

"Right," Invi agreed, quiet yet firm.

Chapter 2

WHEN YOU RETURNED TO DAYBREAK TOWN AFTER your excursion in the Dwarf Woodlands, you spotted an enormous shooting star streaking down through the blue sky.

"Whoa, what's that?" I said, watching it fall as I met you in the Fountain Square. What was going on? "Looks like it fell near the waterfront. Should we go check it out?"

You agreed with a nod. Actually, I realized, you didn't know the town that well. At the center was a fountain, and the bricks laid around it formed a pattern of five stars. There were also loads of houses. And then there was the clocktower off in the distance. It didn't display normal time, though; instead, it had several round clock faces all on top of each other, so it was really hard to read. Its giant pendulum was always swinging. I'd heard the bells even rang once in a while, but only at special times. You probably hadn't heard them yet. And of course, the sky was almost always the color of daybreak. It was a lighter hue than twilight, somewhere between blue and pale violet.

You were hurrying up the steps leading from the square to the waterfront when a Heartless arrived. The pesky creatures had a habit of showing up in the most unexpected places, even in town, but you were already a practiced hand with your Keyblade by that point. Without a moment's hesitation, you took it down. Lux spilled from the Heartless, and you gathered it up before continuing on your way. Collecting this light was your mission as a Keybearer, after all.

You crossed a bridge over one of the many channels carrying clear water around the town and arrived in Waterfront Park, a beautiful green garden facing the sea. You noticed blocks of various colors scattered about the round flower bed at its center.

What were these?

You walked over to one of the blocks and started to pick it up when someone came running toward you.

"*Kupo!*"

It was one of the local Moogle shopkeepers. After locking eyes with you for a moment, the Moogle sharply turned away, apparently embarrassed.

"I smell a munnymaker, *kupo!*" he muttered before snatching up all the blocks in the area and dashing away. You were wondering whether to go after him or not when you heard an unfamiliar, quacking sort of voice: "Aw, phooey! How did this happen?"

"I don't know, Donald. It's like the whole thing just fell apart."

You walked toward the voices and found two figures standing next to an aircraft. By all appearances, it was built of the same type of blocks as the ones lying all over the park.

"Gawrsh!" The taller of the two exclaimed, noticing you. "Is that what I think it is?" He was wearing a yellow hat and pants of the same color, along with a green shirt and brown vest.

The shorter of the two was dressed in blue. "A Keyblade?!" he squawked, and the Heartless chose that moment to make their entrance.

As the two strangers leaped up in surprise, you faced off with the Heartless, Keyblade in hand.

These Heartless were a tad different from the ones you'd encountered before, though; they were shaped like combinations of those blocks. What's more, each time you defeated one of them, instead of the usual Lux, a small block came tumbling out and went flying into the pocket of the tall one.

"*Wak!* What was that?" yelped the short one, peeking into his friend's pocket.

"Got me! Hmm… What's this? Huh?" The tall one pulled the block out of his pocket and inspected it.

"A Gummi block! How did you do that?" the smaller one said in confusion.

Okay, so those things are called Gummi blocks.

"I think maybe it's 'cause of this," the taller one said before removing a small, round device from his pocket—maybe some kind of radar. "When a Gummi Heartless is defeated, this Gummi radar retrieves the Gummi block it was carrying. Of course, we couldn't

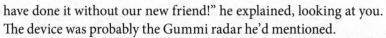

have done it without our new friend!" he explained, looking at you. The device was probably the Gummi radar he'd mentioned.

His short friend was thinking. "Oh. Okay…" After another moment or two of contemplation, he suddenly looked up.

"I'm Donald! And this guy here is…"

"Goofy!"

Once the pair finished introducing themselves to you, you gave them your own name.

"Hey! I almost forgot! Why do *you* have a Keyblade?" Donald asked.

You caught them up to speed.

"Masked figures in white robes?" Donald complained wearily. "Chirithy? What's the big idea?! How come I've never heard of them before?"

"Well, maybe it's because we're someplace new," Goofy commented. "I bet there's still lots we don't know about this world."

"Possibly…" Donald still seemed a little miffed.

Next to him, Goofy gave you a thoughtful look. "Say, maybe you can help us. We came here in a Gummi Ship, but it fell apart when we landed. And then the blocks that the ship was made of were stolen by the Heartless. Do ya think you can help us get 'em back?" he asked, although he sounded extremely hesitant. That aircraft thing in the middle of the park was the Gummi Ship, and the two of them must have ridden it here.

"Goofy! What are you doing?! We don't need help. We can do it on our own," Donald snapped with a hint of annoyance.

"No, we can't, Donald," Goofy pointed out. "Remember, we don't have anything to fight with."

"Oh. Right." Donald hung his head dejectedly.

No two ways about it—the only way to get the blocks back was to take on the Heartless. And that would be almost impossible without weapons.

"So, whaddaya say, pal?" said Goofy. "Do ya think you could collect the Gummi blocks we need?"

"Yeah. It sure would help us." Donald looked up and joined Goofy in asking for your assistance.

You replied with a firm nod.

"Gawrsh, thanks! Oh, and be sure to take this with ya." Goofy placed the Gummi radar in your hand. There were probably plenty of Heartless with plundered Gummi blocks hiding all over town. "We'll be right here tryin' to rebuild the ship with the parts we still have."

With that, you rushed off to help, and the two of them watched you go.

First stop was the boardwalk that ran along the seafront. The Heartless were everywhere, but you started with the Gummi Copters (the aircraft-shaped Heartless like the one you defeated earlier) and took them down left and right.

Eventually, you made it all the way back to the Fountain Square and dealt with the Gummi Copters there, too. But it still wasn't enough. When you forged ahead into the marketplace, you found a Gummi Hammer—a great, round Heartless built from a whole bunch of Gummi blocks. You and your Keyblade were old friends by this point, so the battle was a piece of cake.

After your complete circuit of town, you had quite a collection going.

You returned to Waterfront Park and found Donald and Goofy hanging out by the Gummi Ship, chatting about one thing or another. You called out to them.

"Thanks! You sure found lots of pieces," Goofy said happily.

Donald bobbed his head beside him. "Now let's see if we can put 'em together."

You watched as the duo shuffled around the ship sticking Gummi blocks here and there.

"These pieces fit like this..."

"And this one goes here..."

"*Wak!* Goofy! That doesn't go there!"

As the two began bickering, you started to look a little worried about them.

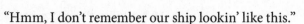

"Hmm, I don't remember our ship lookin' like this."

"Yeah, there's something screwy going on."

The finished Gummi "ship" looked more like a car than anything that could fly.

"Uh, Donald? I don't think that's a spaceship," Goofy sighed.

"*WAK!* What do you mean it's not a— Hey! That's not a spaceship!" Donald snapped back at him. "This is all your fault!" He started taking apart the incorrectly assembled Gummi Ship. "Hmm...looks like we're missing a few blocks for the engine."

"What do we do now...?" Goofy wondered.

Suddenly, you felt the Gummi radar vibrating in your pocket and pulled it out. Goofy peered at its screen with you.

"...Hey, I've never seen a signal like this! Maybe it's the blocks we're missin'."

The radar was directing you back toward the market across the bridge. With a nod, you retraced your steps.

It seemed to you that there were more Heartless with Gummi blocks than before, and you checked the radar again as soon as you got back to the marketplace. All signs pointed to a Heartless with a special block inside one of the neighboring buildings.

You stepped into the dim interior and realized this was probably a warehouse. You found some crates and clambered up to reach the second-floor passageway, where a pitch-black Gummi Copter was lying in ambush.

You readied your Keyblade.

This Heartless was a bit bigger than the ones from earlier, and it fired missiles at you. You jumped out of the way and then hammered the oversize Gummi Copter hovering in the air.

There was a heavy *thud* as your blow hit home and knocked the Heartless to pieces. A Gummi block fell out of it, but this one was shaped differently than the others. You claimed your prize and exited the warehouse.

Now we should be able to fix the Gummi Ship.

However, as soon as you tried to head back, Heartless materialized around you. These ones didn't have Gummi blocks—this type always used magic.

Tense, you brought your Keyblade into fighting position.

Just then a ray of light flashed through the sky, zigzagging down to land right in front of you.

As you jumped back in surprise, someone dressed in red appeared from the light. He was just a bit shorter than you, but he carried himself with dignity and held a Keyblade in his white-gloved hands. He fixed the Heartless with a gaze that was all business. His Keyblade suddenly moved, almost too quickly for you to notice, and then all the Heartless were gone.

"Uh-oh! There's darkness in this world, too...," he said, then turned toward you with a smile. "Oh, and Keyblade wielders."

He extended his hand, and you shook it.

"Hiya, pal. I'm Mickey."

That's right, he was Mickey Mouse. Now that introductions were out of the way, Mickey let go of your hand and frowned.

"It looks like I took a surprise journey to a new world." He took a moment to get a look at his surroundings. "Say, have you seen my friends Donald and Goofy? They would have appeared outta the sky just like me."

You had, of course, so you filled Mickey in on everything that had happened.

"Their ship was destroyed? And you're helping them rebuild it? Gosh, thanks! Guess it's a lucky thing I landed here," he said, and then glanced over his shoulder. "Of course, I never would have made it without my two copilots."

He appeared to be speaking to someone behind him, but you couldn't see anyone there...

"Your Majesty!" Suddenly, two little chipmunks popped up over Mickey's shoulders. Wait, was Mickey a king?

The two chipmunks hopped down to the ground.

"Remind me to show you how to use the brakes next time!" the one with the black nose complained.

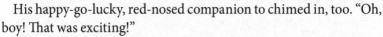

His happy-go-lucky, red-nosed companion to chimed in, too. "Oh, boy! That was exciting!"

"Sorry, Chip. Sorry, Dale. It's just that I was in a hurry," Mickey apologized. Chip and Dale must have been their names. "Now I've gotta go look into something. Fellas, would you two go and give Donald and Goofy a hand?" the king asked in a cheerful voice.

"Leave it to us!" declared Chip proudly.

"Say, pal, would you show them the way?"

After you agreed to Mickey's request, Chip and Dale jumped onto your shoulders. "Thanks!"

You hurried to Waterfront Park, where Donald and Goofy were waiting.

Mickey watched you all go, then looked up at the sky. "So it wasn't the Star Shard that led me here. Hmm… What exactly is going on?" he muttered to himself.

Meanwhile, one of the Foretellers was watching him.

"And just what are you doing here…?"

You arrived at Waterfront Park, clearing out Heartless every step of the way.

Donald and Goofy had rebuilt the Gummi Ship, and this time, it was a real, working ship—as if they planned to go sailing.

"Wow! This is neat!" squeaked Dale. You had to agree, it didn't look half bad, but…

"No, it's not! It's not neat! It's a disaster! How did this happen?!" Chip exclaimed in horror at the mixed-up Gummi Ship.

"I don't know. Chip, what do you think?" Goofy said slowly as he turned in the chipmunk's direction. "Huh? Chip! Dale! You're here!" He hurried over to them.

"What?!" Donald waddled after him.

"Sit back and relax, fellas!" declared Chip as Dale bounced up onto Donald's head.

"Yeah, leave this to us!"

They dashed over to the vehicle and gave it a look. Those two sure knew their way around a Gummi Ship.

"The frame is perfect, but we're missing a core part!" Dale stated.

The core... Didn't we have something like that?

You showed everyone the black Gummi block you found in the warehouse.

"Ya mean that one?" Goofy said, pointing at the block.

"Yep!" Chip said as he took it from you.

"This'll only take a second!"

Chip and Dale began reassembling the Gummi Ship.

"Gawrsh, that's a relief." Goofy grinned at you.

"And it's all because of you! Thanks!" exclaimed Donald happily.

"But hey, where did ya meet Chip and Dale?"

You told Goofy about your encounter with Mickey.

"The king!"

"His Majesty is here?!"

Donald and Goofy shared a joyful glance.

That was when Chip shouted, "Ta-daa!"

The chipmunks had put the Gummi Ship back together into something that resembled a plane. At last, it looked like it could fly.

"You better check the engine," Chip cautioned Donald and Goofy before they climbed onboard. He waited on top of the craft with Dale.

"It's this button, right?" Donald said, punching it without waiting for an answer.

"Donald! No!"

"Huh?"

While Goofy panicked, the Gummi Ship almost instantly began shuddering.

Chip and Dale hopped up and down in alarm.

"What's happening?" Dale asked, rather nonchalantly given the situation.

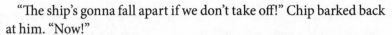

"The ship's gonna fall apart if we don't take off!" Chip barked back at him. "Now!"

The Gummi Ship's engine revved higher and higher, ready to take flight at any moment.

"But what about the king?"

The question was barely out of Dale's mouth when Mickey came running over. The king flashed you a smile and then hopped aboard, while Chip and Dale slid from the roof into the cockpit after him.

"C'mon, it's time to go home—to our world."

As if it had been waiting for him to give the okay, the Gummi Ship blasted off.

All you could do was watch them go in stunned silence.

That's when I appeared next to you with a flip in the air and joined you in watching the king and his friends vanish into the sky.

"They were a friendly, noisy bunch, weren't they?" I murmured, still looking up. "So *he's* the king."

You stood there beside me for a while, gazing up into the canvas of dawn above.

The gears turned noisily within the clocktower in Daybreak Town, as they always did. They fit together so perfectly that they almost formed a solid wall, and next to that wall was a desk. The flasks scattered across the top suggested someone was conducting research here.

The Master of Masters sat before the desk in his black coat, flipping through the pages of a book. Nearby was a young man dressed exactly the same, named Luxu. It was difficult to get a good look at his face because of his hood.

"So that makes you the indispensable number seven," the Master commented in his usual flippant tone.

"Sure..." Luxu wasn't entirely sure how to respond to that.

"Come on! It's simple. You six plus me is seven," said the Master. Suddenly, his head snapped toward Luxu as he realized something. "Wait. Don't tell me I don't count!"

"No... Uh, um..."

The Master of Masters stood up before his confused apprentice, sauntered over to stand directly in front of him, and stuck out his right hand. In it appeared a Keyblade—the nameless Keyblade that would eventually be passed down to a certain man.

"Here, take it."

The Master of Masters approached Luxu to begin the Bequeathing. Beside the Master was a black box.

Everything yet to come would be tied to the role Luxu received here, but that was a tale for the distant future. For now, no one knew.

Chapter 3

KINGDOM HEARTS X [chi]

UPON RETURNING TO DAYBREAK TOWN AFTER A MIS-
sion, you stopped by one of the Moogle shops to see if there was
anything that might come in handy.

"Well, well. Another wielder," said a boy who was also picking up
a few supplies. He had a Keyblade, too, and so did two other customers. You got the feeling that the three of them knew each other. "Have
you heard? A new breed of Heartless has been spotted all over town."

You shook your head.

"Sounds like they're a handful. We're thinking of splitting up and
thinning them out. Care to help?"

You accepted. After all, four Keyblades were way better than one.

"We're all meeting back here when we're done with our share.
Good luck out there!"

With that, the other Keyblade wielders left.

"*Kupo!*" one of the Moogles added. "If there's some hardy Heartless roaming about, then you'd better come prepared, *kupo!*" Maybe
he'd already forgotten about how he snatched those Gummi blocks
away from you not so long ago.

You bought what you needed and left the shop.

Everything seemed normal in town—no sign of the new Heartless
for the moment. Where could they be lurking?

You started your search by heading first for Waterfront Park, taking
out the usual Heartless along the way. Some of them were stronger
than normal, you noticed, but you had help now. Most of the time you
fought on your own, but it was kind of nice to have some friends to
share the action with.

You did a circuit of the whole town, absorbed in your Heartless hunt.

Still, why were there so many Heartless in Daybreak Town in the
first place?

While you were busy fending off the Heartless—

I was doing a little solo sky-gazing in one of the quieter parts of Daybreak Town when I was joined by another me—another Chirithy.

"Hi, Chirithy," I said, and the other me answered in kind.

"Hi, Chirithy."

The two of us were identical in every way, from our appearance to our behavior, voice, and mannerisms.

"So how's your wielder?" I asked him.

"Indifferent."

"Oh…," I responded with an understanding nod.

"I don't think he understands what's going on."

"He'll learn. He has to."

"You're right. There are only five unions."

"…And we can't afford to lose any of them, which is why we need to trust our wielders will flourish."

After our hushed conversation was over, we looked up at the sky. It was the same predawn color as always…

With the Heartless a thing of the past, you returned to the Moogle's shop.

But the Keyblade wielders you'd agreed to work with were nowhere to be seen. In their place was a Chirithy. You searched for your friends, but could find neither hide nor hair of them. The Chirithy in the shop seemed just the slightest bit different from your constant companion—which would be me. You weren't sure what exactly felt off about him.

Suddenly, the Chirithy quietly told you, "He's not coming…"

The words came as a shock. You had an arrangement, so why couldn't he come?

"…But he left you a message," the Chirithy continued. "'I'm sorry I couldn't keep our promise.' That's it. Hafta go!"

His message delivered, the Chirithy did the usual flip and vanished in a puff of smoke.

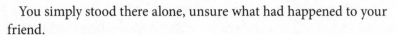

You simply stood there alone, unsure what had happened to your friend.

And then—

A few days later, I was in the same spot where I'd talked with other Chirithy, beneath the dawn sky in a corner of Daybreak Town with a view of the clocktower. This time, though, the other me was lying weak and exhausted on the ground.

He offered a feeble greeting when I approached. "Hi, Chirithy."

"…What's wrong?" I replied, a little saddened.

"My Keyblade wielder disappeared into darkness… Is this the end?" he asked. I wondered if he was referring to your friend. Maybe it was someone else. "We have a connection to our Keyblade wielders. If they disappear, so do we," he told me. He was trying to warn me, I think.

"Yeah…"

I knew exactly what he was talking about, but I had nothing better to say than that. I sat up and directed my gaze toward the sky. It was that same familiar color.

In front of me, the fallen Chirithy floated into the air. Up and up he rose, until he gradually faded from view.

All I could do was watch.

We meet the same fate as the ones we guide—if they disappear, then that's what happens to us, too.

His Keyblade wielder was lost to the darkness.

It was a fearsome force we were fighting. I had no way of knowing if or when you might vanish, too, which was scary to think about.

After the other me had completely faded from sight, Invi the Fore-teller appeared behind me.

"The wielders are gathering Lux at an extraordinary pace," she said. "However, the darkness is spreading even faster."

I spun around toward her. Choosing my words carefully, I asked her a question. "Then…there really is a traitor among the five?"

"I'm not willing to believe that yet," the Foreteller said in a subdued voice, and then we both looked up toward where the Chirithy had vanished.

What happened? Why didn't he come? you wondered to yourself as you walked around the streets of Daybreak Town alone. The Heartless you faced earlier were fierce. A shudder ran through you as you imagined the worst. If you didn't get stronger, there was no telling when you would start breaking promises, too.

You had to get stronger.

Your grip on your Keyblade tightened.

Much stronger.

Nearby, I appeared with my little flip from a puff of smoke—except it wasn't actually me. Still, I'm sure you thought it was.

"You're making amazing progress! I could tell you had potential from day one. But what if I told you…I had something to make you even stronger?"

He was right; you'd just been thinking about that.

You nodded, and Chirithy peered into the pouch hanging from his neck.

"Let's see here… Dun-dada-duuun!" he said with a showman's flair as he removed his gift from the purse. It was a pretty bracelet, embedded with a star-shaped stone. "Check out this Power Bangle!"

You accepted the bracelet and put it on your arm. The sparkling Power Bangle fit so comfortably that it was hard to believe you'd only just put it on. You were so pleased you couldn't help but show it off.

A hard-to-read expression appeared on the other Chirithy's face—an expression I never would have made. "Yep, looks great. Moving on," he said, jumping right into the next topic. "Just keep this little bangle on, and you can collect something called 'Guilt' from the Heartless you defeat. You can use Guilt to get even stronger—although you won't get it every time."

"Guilt"—this was new. Your lowered your head in thought. Wasn't guilt that awful feeling you got when you did something wrong? How do you collect it from Heartless to boost your own abilities?

"Don't look at me like that. Come on, give it a shot. It won't be so bad! And the best part is, it's a gift! The bangle is yours to keep. Well, if you really want to do something in return, then…just keep it equipped and continue to do what you're doing. I hope it'll motivate you to get out there and do even better!"

He had a point—you'd be able to collect Lux for your Union and Guilt for yourself at the same time. Two birds, one stone.

You held your Keyblade aloft, telling him you would.

"I knew I could count on you. Good luck!" the Chirithy said cheerily, and then did a flip and vanished in midair just like I would.

So of course you didn't realize I was never there.

After you set out for the next world, you arrived in a small chamber. This was Wonderland. You didn't see anything out of the ordinary, just a solitary table with a small bottle atop it in the middle of the room. Well, there was *one* odd thing—you couldn't find the exit.

You did spot a small door eventually, but you wouldn't be fitting through that anytime soon. It would've been a really tight squeeze even for me.

You squatted down to get a better look at the door. Then—

"Looking for a way out, I suppose."

The doorknob talked! You drew your hand back in surprise.

"Sorry, you're much too big. Simply impassable."

But by all appearances, this door was the only way out of here.

As you tried to come up with some kind of idea, the doorknob hurriedly added, "Oh no. You're not going to cry, are you? Crying won't help." It closed its eyes for a moment as if trying to remember something. "Hmm…but perhaps this will. A girl visited earlier. Why don't you talk to her? She may have some advice."

You tilted your head to one side inquisitively.

"Where is she, you ask? Why, on the other side. Naturally."

With no other options, you reached for the doorknob, but this time, it glowered angrily at you.

"No, no, no. As I said, you're simply much too big. Of course, there's always another way." The doorknob looked over at the table. "Why don't you try the bottle on the table? Read the directions, and directly you'll be directed in the right direction. And then— Wait, you have a key! Well, why didn't you say so? Now all you need—"

But just as you stood up to look at the table yourself, a mysterious shadow snatched up the bottle and ran off.

It was a Heartless!

"Oh, that's rather unfortunate."

The doorknob urged you to get it back, and you gave chase with Keyblade in hand. Unfortunately, the little thief was quite agile, and it stayed just out of reach as it darted all over the tiny room. You chased it over the sofa, onto the shelves, under the table, and pretty much everywhere else before you were finally able to catch it and get the bottle back.

There was a red label affixed to the neck of the bottle, a drawing of a big tree becoming small.

"I wonder if this is a good idea…," I thought aloud, but you simply nodded, brought the bottle to your lips, and took a big gulp. A few seconds later, you were tiny. You seemed okay, so I took a drink from the bottle myself. *Hmm, tastes funny.* Next thing I knew, I was shrunk, too.

We shared a laugh and then headed for the little door.

You touched the doorknob only to find that it was locked. The doorknob itself wasn't very chatty this time, either. There was only one way to handle this—you held your Keyblade to the keyhole, a beam of light fired out, and there was a *click*.

We stepped through the door.

* * *

Beyond lay a lush, green forest.

"Now what's all this?" I asked, confused.

You responded with a shrug and started walking off. These woods were full of oddly shaped trees, but there were still clear paths to follow. We came across a lone girl at a fork in the road. She had gold hair and wore a blue dress with a white apron.

"Why, hello there. My name is Alice. Who might you be?" the girl asked, and you introduced yourself, too. "Oh? Thank goodness! I was afraid you'd speak in riddles, too."

Riddles? What does she mean?

"I don't suppose you've seen a white rabbit, have you? I've been looking for him everywhere."

You shook your head.

"I see. How unfortunate. Now, where could he have gone?" Alice said, then paused to think.

And that just so happened to be the moment when a peculiar white rabbit in glasses dashed by the two of you in a terrible hurry, clutching a watch in his paws. "I'm late! I'm late! For a very important date! No time to say hello. Good-bye! I'm late, I'm late, I'm late!"

"Why, there he is!" Alice cried, giving chase. This was the very rabbit she'd told you about. "Wait! Please! Mr. Rabbit!"

You were about to go after her when you heard another voice behind you. "Lose something? Your way, perhaps?"

You looked back to find a talking cat, a very curious creature with pink and purple stripes.

…Well, I'm kind of like a talking cat myself, so maybe I don't have room to judge.

"Or an answer? I've lots of those. The questions don't matter, of course. All answers here have lots of questions. Alice went after the White Rabbit, but who's asking?"

You and I shared a glance. I mean, we just saw! What a weirdo!

The two of us hurried off after Alice instead. We searched around the forest for a little while, when…

"Help!" The rabbit from before came running in our direction. "A monster! Help! Assistance!" he shouted as he kept on going right past us.

What if he was talking about a Heartless? We went up the path he'd come from and found a clearing in the forest.

There stood a house with a red roof and one giant problem—Alice's arms and legs were sticking out from the doors and windows, and her face was peeking out of a second-floor window.

In this state, someone could easily mistake her for a monster.

Did she suddenly get bigger? we wondered.

"Oh dear…," she said, her eyes welling with tears.

That was when the Heartless arrived. Alice wouldn't be going anywhere like this, so you squared off against them. They liked to use fire spells, but you fended off their magic as you took them down, taking care not to let the flames reach the surrounding trees.

Once you had finished dealing with the last of them, you turned around and grinned at Alice.

"That's better," she sighed. "At least now I shan't be burnt. Oh, but whatever shall I do about my…unusual size?"

We were all racking our brains over that very question when Alice spotted something nearby.

"Why look! A garden! Perhaps if I ate something, I'd return to my regular size. Oh, but I can't quite reach it. Would you kindly gather some vegetables for me?"

With a nod, you picked some ripe carrots and fed them to Alice. They did the trick, and she shrank right back down again.

"Thank you!" Alice said with a bob of her head as she burst out of the house, happy as can be—and then she immediately took off after the White Rabbit again. "Oh no, wait! Please, wait! Mr. Rabbit!"

"What a weird world," I remarked, and you laughed.

*　　*　　*

That night, you had a dream.

There were six people in a room, apparently inside the clocktower. You knew one of them—Master Invi, the leader of your Union. Four of the others wore masks of different animals, so you guessed that they were the Foretellers.

The masked five were listening to the sixth as he gave a speech to them, but you had no idea who he was.

All you knew was that this dream was going to lead you to actions, and those actions would change the course of your future.

When you woke up in the familiar comfort of your room, I was worriedly watching you from beside your bed. "That must've been some dream. You were tossing and turning like crazy," I said.

You couldn't remember anything about what you saw, except that it was about something you didn't know.

"Close your eyes and try to get some sleep," I told you softly, and you drifted off again. Once I was sure you were snoring quietly again, I spoke to someone outside the window. Another Chirithy. "Was that you?"

He poked his head inside and said, "Did you show him the dream?" I didn't reply, so the Chirithy outside the window asked me another question. "What is it you're trying to do?" Maybe it was just my imagination, but this other me looked just a shade grayer.

"The opposite of what you're doing," I answered.

The other Chirithy thought for a moment. "I guess that makes us enemies," he said, melting away into the gloom of the night. I watched him go, then turned back to your sleeping face.

"Don't worry. I'll protect you. I have to...," I whispered.

The next morning, you woke up without any memory of the dream and headed for the Fountain Square.

"Hey! *Kupo!*"

A Moogle came rushing out of his shop with some news for you.

"Help! There's a big, scary monster in Waterfront Park, *kupo*! It's frightening away all my customers! If I have to close up shop, my regulars will be lost, *kupo*! Can you take care of it? Please, *kupo*?"

Once the Moogle finished foisting his problems off on you, he scurried back into his shop.

Still…if he went to the trouble of asking you, maybe he actually had more faith in your abilities than he did in the other Keyblade wielders.

You left the Fountain Square for Waterfront Park, and there, in the exact same spot where you met Donald and Goofy, was a Heartless you had never seen before—a giant, pitch-black Invisible with enormous wings.

There was also a boy with a Keyblade like yours facing off with the Heartless. He had silver hair, and he wore a black jacket over a white shirt with a red scarf around his neck.

He sprang into the air and dealt the Invisible a swift blow with his Keyblade. You could tell just from watching him move that your skills had nothing on his. With one final strike, the boy vanquished the Invisible.

But only a second later, he nearly collapsed right then and there. You hurried over to him and called out.

The boy looked up with a wince of pain. "I'm all right," he said.

You lent him a hand as he tried to get to his feet.

"I'm Ephemer. I belong to the Union Unicornis. Nice to meet you!"

You responded in kind, telling him your name and the Union to which you belonged.

"Looks like we're on different teams," Ephemer commented, noticing your Union name.

You nodded back. This was your first time meeting a member of a different Union…or was it? You hadn't heard the names or the Unions of the other wielders you'd met in the shop that day, you remembered sadly.

"But I'm working on something other than my Union task today, so think of me as Union-free for the day," Ephemer added. He must

have misread the melancholy in your expression as distrust for the wielders of other Unions.

Anyway, what did he mean by "something other than my Union task"? Your head tilted curiously to the side.

"Hmm," murmured Ephemer, trying to decide what to say. "I guess I can tell you what it is, since you helped me out. Can you keep a secret?" He took a step closer and continued. "The worlds we visit—the worlds of fairy tales—are nothing more than holograms. You know, projections. The light we collect there is actually this world's light."

The revelation went right over your head. Fairy tales? Holograms?? Projections???

You were obviously confused, so Ephemer fell into thought and walked a short distance away. "Um..."

Another moment of contemplation, and then he spoke up again.

"To put it simply: There are lots of worlds, right? And they're all connected by land. But it's impossible to go around all of them. That's why there's a mechanism that projects those worlds here and allows us to collect Lux from faraway lands."

You didn't quite understand, but you were starting to sense that whatever Ephemer was talking about was extremely important. You nodded enthusiastically anyway.

"I'm gathering information, trying to figure out how the whole thing works. My hunch is that the Book of Prophecies held by the Foretellers is what's creating these holograms."

But the more he explained, the more confused you got.

"Get it? Or have I lost you?"

You knew Ephemer was telling you something big, but you couldn't quite get your head around the implications.

This involved the Foretellers, the Book of Prophecies, and projections of worlds?

You understood the Foretellers and Book of Prophecies well enough. It was the part about the worlds being holograms that had you stumped.

Ephemer had paused, maybe to see if you were still with him, and then kept talking. "Anyway, we're in this town, gathering the light that belongs to this vast world. Not just gathering, fighting over it, without knowing why. After a little digging, I discovered that all the Unions have different goals."

That was when last night's dream came rushing back to you all at once.

You remembered that room where the five Foretellers had been, and if Ephemer was right about the Union leaders being after different things…?

You began to wonder if that had really been a dream at all.

"What is it?" Ephemer asked, noticing your reaction. You told him what you'd seen, and he lapsed into a contemplative silence as he listened. "Really? Interesting… Hey, I've got an idea. Why don't you come with me?"

You decided to say yes. If that vision was showing you something real, of course you wanted to know more.

"Great! Then let's head to the place you saw in your dream."

Ephemer looked at the clocktower in the distance. Right—whatever you saw had happened in there.

Once you and Ephemer had left, I appeared in the vacant park.

But I wasn't the only one keeping an eye on you.

"Is he yours?" I asked. Unable to hide, the other Chirithy from the night before revealed himself.

"I don't know, is he?" he retorted. Whatever the real answer was, I doubt he would have told me. Just as I wasn't about to tell him why I showed you that dream.

"You're not the same color you were before," I commented. I couldn't believe it; he was so dark now.

"Very perceptive. So what's your next move? They're getting closer to the truth. Are you going to allow that?"

I didn't answer; my gaze just followed you and Ephemer to the clocktower.

*   *   *

The two of you arrived at the base of the great tower.

"So you don't know where the room is?" Ephemer asked, and you shook your head. "I've been here a few times, but I haven't found a way in."

The tower was apparently designed to keep out all but the most determined. You looked up at it, slightly dismayed.

"All right, let's split up," Ephemer suggested, "and see if we can get inside somehow."

That sounded like a good idea to you.

"Okay, I'll go check over by the bridge," Ephemer said, already heading over. "You go see if there's some other place we can get in."

You decided to start with the front door, just in case, but it wouldn't open. You gave the problem a little more thought.

A way you could get inside... This seaside town was full of canals, which led to the clocktower. Maybe following one of them would provide you with the entrance you needed.

Oh, right—there were stairs leading down to the canals from the Fountain Square.

You made that your first stop, disposing of the Heartless that popped up along the way. If you remembered correctly, there was a small passage partway down the stairs from the square to Waterfront Park.

You descended the narrow steps to a waterway that had run dry, and inside it was a manhole that led underground.

Once you dispatched the Heartless hovering almost protectively over it, you climbed into the hole and down the ladder. At the bottom was a dark sewer, stuffy and humid. As you headed deeper, you could see water flowing down from overhead like a waterfall along several gears turning together. Ephemer came running up from behind.

"Great minds think alike," he quipped as he surveyed the area. "Other than the entrance, this is the only place that connects outside. Be careful, there's a fair share of Heartless around here."

The two of you ran through the sewers, which turned out to be even more infested with Heartless than the streets above. Still, you kept pressing onward—until you met an Invisible.

Directly in your path was the same kind of Heartless as the one Ephemer had fought earlier, hovering near the ceiling. There was also a door visible just past it.

You got your Keyblade ready. Even if Ephemer had managed to beat one, this Heartless was no joke. Fortunately, you weren't on your own here.

You sprang at the Invisible, chopping at it with your Keyblade, only to be knocked away by its sword. Ephemer was sent tumbling across the ground next to you, too. You got your Keyblade back into position and lunged again. If attacking from above was no good, then this time you would come in low.

You swung your Keyblade upward at the Heartless's legs, but its sword was already coming for you. Just then, Ephemer darted forward, launched himself into the air, and landed a full combo. You quickly followed with a rising strike from your own Keyblade.

The combined damage from your Keyblades hit home, and the Invisible dispersed into black smoke.

Ephemer turned to you, out of breath but beaming. "Now we're even," he said, and you heard the door opening.

You rushed over to it, but then Ephemer stopped you.

"Wait."

You turned back toward him.

"I think we should come back later."

The suggestion was surprising, especially since you had worked so hard to find this entrance.

"It's taken us this long just to find a way in," said Ephemer. "Think of how much longer it'll take for us to enter the tower and find the room. It's gonna look suspicious to our Union leaders if we're missing for too long. We know how to get in now. Let's save the rest for another day."

He had a point. It had taken you quite a while to get to this passage, so maybe calling it a day here was for the best.

You nodded in agreement.

"We may not be in the same Union, but we're friends, right?" Ephemer grinned and held out his hand. You quickly offered yours as well, and the two of you shook on it. "Let's meet tomorrow at the Fountain Square. How about noon?"

The idea brought a smile to your face.

After that, the two of you retraced your steps back to the surface.

It was night, and you were back in your room, lying in bed thinking about the boy you'd met. I was over by the window, where I usually spent my evenings with you.

"Someone looks happy," I commented. "Tell me, tell me!"

As you told me all about Ephemer, just listening to you made me happy, too.

"You made a new friend? That's great! No wonder you're smiling. I hear having friends is nice. But I wouldn't know because I don't have any."

You looked a little upset and pointed at yourself.

"Huh? You?" I asked, and you nodded back at me.

I found myself feeling slightly bashful. "You're my friend...? Oh, ha-ha."

You chuckled a little, too.

It had never occurred to me that a familiar could be friends with his Keyblade wielder, but now that I thought about it, maybe that's what we actually were.

—Meanwhile, Ephemer was standing in the sewers alone before the door. He'd chosen not to go through with his new friend.

"Sorry...," he whispered, slipping into the tower through the door he'd found with that very same friend.

*　　*　　*

The next day, you went to the Fountain Square, killing time by yourself until Ephemer would arrive—but he never did. You waited and waited and waited, but to no avail.

"Have you been here all day?" I said to you. You were too disappointed to reply. "Come on, let's head home."

At my suggestion, you lowered your gaze. I knew what you wanted to say: *I have to be here when Ephemer comes.*

"Look. I'm sure something important came up."

You raised your head and shot me a look.

You were remembering the other Keyblade wielder who hadn't come back—the one who had promised to hunt Heartless with you. You still hadn't crossed paths.

"A friend always keeps their promise. Maybe he had an emergency. You should give him the benefit of the doubt."

Though you got to your feet, you still moved very slowly. I could tell you really wanted to wait. You trusted him, but you were worried that the same thing that had happened to your other friend had happened to him—and maybe he was never coming back.

"Don't be sad. When you're sad, it makes me sad, too."

I walked up to you slowly and squeezed your hand with my own tiny one.

You swept me up into a tight hug.

The Master of Masters stood on a hill overlooking Daybreak Town. Behind him was a young man in a unicorn mask—Ira. He was tall, and the skirt of his white robe was the blue of an early morning sky. Atop his hood was a blue unicorn's mane.

"So, did you look through the Book?" asked the Master of Masters.

"Yes. But I'm still analyzing it," replied Ira quietly.

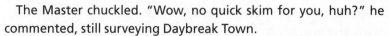

The Master chuckled. "Wow, no quick skim for you, huh?" he commented, still surveying Daybreak Town.

"I just prefer to be thorough," said Ira behind him. "Master, is what it says in the last passage true?"

"Oh yeah, that. Bummer, huh?" The Master of Masters sounded almost cheerful, but Ira was not.

"...Yes."

"By the way, if one day I suddenly disappear, I'm countin' on you to keep the others calm. Okay?"

Ira raised his head. "Huh? Dis...appear?"

"Vanish? Dim? Fade? I don't know how to explain it. It's just hypothetical talk," the Master of Masters elaborated as he watched the sun set on Daybreak Town.

"Okay...," Ira agreed, though obviously shaken.

"This world is full of light. It's a world comprised of many smaller worlds, all connected, stretching as far as the eye can see. One great light protects us all throughout this vast land. All worlds share one light, one fate," he told Ira, his voice unusually soft.

"I take it you're talking about Kingdom Hearts," Ira replied.

"Yep! You're right on the money. People believe that the light that is Kingdom Hearts will be here forever. But if it were to disappear, the world would be enveloped in darkness."

It was an ominous thing to hear from his teacher.

"I understand," Ira said. "And that is why you granted us these Keyblades. With these we can spread the teachings of light, and we can protect Kingdom Hearts from darkness—"

"No, they're not for protecting Kingdom Hearts," the Master of Masters interrupted.

"Huh?"

Once again solemn, the Master quoted a line from the Book of Prophecies. "The final passage reads, 'On that fated land, a great war shall transpire. Darkness will prevail and the light expire.'"

"Isn't it our duty as Keyblade wielders to prevent this war from taking place?" his student asked back.

The Master stretched his arms over his head, almost playfully. "Nah, not possible."

"Wha—?" Ira could not hide his surprise at such a blunt reply.

"You really think you can change the future?" the Master of Masters chided, as if his student should know this already.

A bit nonplussed, Ira asked yet another question: "Then...what do you want us to do?"

"We have to focus on what comes after," the Master explained, a little more gently this time. "There's no use thinking of ways to change events we know are gonna happen."

Still, Ira wasn't satisfied. "But what about all of those who are here now? And the ones who will be here when the darkness finally comes? Are we to abandon all of them?"

The Master of Masters barked an exasperated laugh at that. "C'mon, are you telling me that you think the world can be saved by just seven people?" He watched as Ira hung his head, searching desperately for an answer.

"We have to at least try! With enough Keyblade wielders we could..."

"Well, if you wanna give it a shot...," the Master offered.

"Yes," replied Ira earnestly.

"All righty, good luck!" the Master of Masters said. The reply came so quickly, it was as if he already knew what his student would say.

Before them, the darkness of night settled over Daybreak Town.

Chapter 4

FOR A LITTLE WHILE AFTER I WAS BORN, THERE WAS still only one of me, and I spent my time sleeping in the Master's flask. I was too drowsy to do much of anything else.

On one of those days, everyone was staring at me inside my glass home.

"Oh, right, before I forget...," said the Master, "if a wielder is overcome by malice—or rather, if their heart is tainted by darkness—their adorable little Spirit will turn dark and become a Nightmare."

Ira's head snapped up. "So you're telling us that if we see a Nightmare...," he began uneasily.

Invi, still wearing her snake mask, finished his thought. "Someone has fallen to darkness."

"Exactly," the Master replied. His voice was just a smidge more serious than usual. "And if you don't stop this renegade Spirit, it'll plant darkness in the hearts of others, and you'll have an army of Nightmares on your hands. Beware."

"So, if we see one of these Nightmares anywhere, we have to get rid of it on the spot," Aced declared definitively.

"No! I won't let you do that!" Ava shielded me where I slept in my bottle. Not that *I* was a Nightmare.

"No wonder you ended up as the bear. You're scary," Gula interjected casually, before the situation could get too uncomfortable.

"Your point?" Aced retorted uncertainly.

Ava grinned. "Maybe you can growl at them?"

"Don't insult me!" he barked back at her.

But then the Master stepped in—and poured more fuel on the fire. "Come on, Aced. You won't know if it works unless you try!" he said, dissolving into giggles.

"Please tell me you're joking."

It seemed the Master's poor attempt at smoothing things out had cooled Aced's temper anyway, and with the tension gone, everyone shared a laugh. It would probably be the first and last time I saw them all having a good time together.

*   *   *

I remember something else that happened, a few days before you met Ephemer.

The Foretellers had assembled in a room of the clocktower at the behest of their leader, Ira.

"There's a traitor among us," he declared once they had all arrived. It was hard to tell if anyone there was surprised—the masks concealed any emotions that might have slipped.

"Are you certain? What proof do you have?" Invi was the first to speak up.

Ira summoned an image of a black Chirithy above the palm of his hand. "I found this sniffing around."

"Is that...a dark Chirithy?" Ava asked uncertainly, while Invi froze.

"Is that...a Nightmare?" It was the word they were dreading.

All eyes went to Ira.

"...It's not me."

Aced broke the silence. He was probably remembering the jokes from when the Chirithy came into the world.

"There's an easy way to solve this. If we all summon our Spirits, then we'll know," suggested Gula softly.

But Invi calmly shot down his idea. "Unfortunately, there are countless wielders in our Unions. It would be easy for us to summon a Chirithy that isn't a Nightmare. I'm afraid that your suggestion wouldn't help us get to the bottom of this."

She was right; there were as many Chirithies out there as there were Keybearers. No one could argue with Invi's levelheaded reminder.

"Yeah, in that case, who's to say that the Nightmare you saw belongs to one of us? It could belong to anyone in our Unions," said Ava, unable to bear the distrust brewing between them.

"That's highly unlikely," Ira said, brushing aside the notion. "Do you recall the tool the wielders were given in order to make them

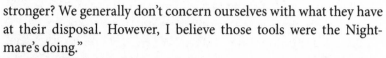

stronger? We generally don't concern ourselves with what they have at their disposal. However, I believe those tools were the Nightmare's doing."

Ira was referring to the Power Bangles.

"The bangles? I know when they're equipped, they have the power to collect dark energy, but I thought we all agreed that was okay." Ava desperately tried to argue, but it wasn't enough for Ira.

"Collecting is fine. But using that power is the equivalent of using the power of darkness."

"It's a brilliant plan. Everyone knows that all the spirits look the same, and wielders exist in spades. There's no way to tell," Gula mused.

"Oh no. Everyone's already equipped their bangles."

Ava was on the verge of tears; beneath her mask, she might have already started crying.

Aced took a step toward Ira. "So now what? How do we find out who's behind this?" he demanded, but Ira kept his cool.

"Seeing as those bangles couldn't have been acquired by just anyone, I believe it's one of us here in this room." It sounded like he'd already decided there was a traitor, so Invi stepped in before he could take it too far.

"No, Ira. I respectfully disagree. What proof do we have that the bangles are tied to the power of darkness, or if a Nightmare is to blame? We shouldn't simply jump to conclusions."

She was trying to call everyone back to their senses, but Aced had more to say. "Ira. Some leader you are. You've managed to plant seeds of doubt in all of us with that speech. What? Did you expect the traitor to give themselves up with that accusation of yours? That was foolish."

"Aced, that's quite enough," said Invi in an attempt to calm the situation. Ava lowered her gaze, while Gula was lost in thought. Meanwhile, Ira was peering at the other four suspiciously, trying to suss out who was the culprit.

"It looks to me like the Master made the wrong choice," Aced spat. As if he couldn't stand to spend another minute with them, he turned his back on the other Foretellers and stormed off.

Invi tried to stop him—"Wait. Where do you think you're going?"—but Aced didn't even look back.

"I think we're done here. I trust you'll keep us all updated," Gula quipped in his usual affable tone, a stark contrast to Aced's angry accusations, before he left, too.

Ava watched them go, lifting her head. "I hope… I hope we can all resolve this soon…," she murmured, bowing briefly to Ira and then taking her leave herself.

The only two still there were Ira and Invi.

"That didn't go as expected," the leader of the Foretellers said with a sigh.

"What's wrong, Ira?" Invi asked. "This isn't like you."

He raised his head slightly and said, "A lost page…"

That got Invi's attention.

"Something's missing from our Book of Prophecies," Ira explained. "Each of our copies were said to contain the events of the future. But this incident, well, it's nowhere to be found."

"And how does this whole thing with the traitor tie together?"

Ira responded to her question by taking up his own Book of Prophecies and opening it. "Like I said, it's nowhere to be found… in my Book."

"Ira, are you implying that someone is in possession of the missing page? And the person with the complete Book is the traitor?"

Ira nodded at Invi as she arrived at one possible answer.

A Lost Page, and a traitor.

At this point, the identity of this mysterious double-crosser was still unknown to everyone.

"There is something going on, and a page is suspiciously missing from the Book. It's not so far-fetched to assume that the one who has the lost page has been turned, that they have fallen into the hands of darkness. Trust me."

Invi opened her own copy of the Book of Prophecies. "There

seems to be no record of it in my Book, either. You may be onto something." She paused a moment, still unsure, then cast a glance at Ira. "I wonder… Could this have been the Master's plan all along? To grant the Lost Page to only one of us."

"We have no way of knowing," Ira instantly replied, and a hint of sadness crept into his voice. "The Master is gone."

That's right, the Master was gone. He had vanished, dimmed, faded.

No one knew his whereabouts. It was entirely possible that he was truly gone for good.

Invi spoke again, as much to dispel the gloom as anything else. "I understand what you are saying. I promise to keep a close eye on the others. I will keep you informed, as always."

"Thanks."

"Of course. After all, that is what the Master asked of me," Invi said. She started to walk away, but then came to a halt, turned back to Ira, and offered one more bit of advice. "And Ira, may your heart be your guiding key."

Now let's jump ahead to a few days later—to the day you met Ephemer.

Aced, Ava, and Gula were together in a warehouse in Daybreak Town. Aced, the eldest of the three, was speaking to the younger two.

"I was wrong about Ira," he said. "I thought he would make a great leader, but he let me down."

Gula didn't seem particularly troubled—he never did—while Ava appeared somewhat dispirited.

"Well, what do you two think? You don't believe what Ira said, do you?"

Gula was the first to reply. "Of course not. His argument was unconvincing. It's like Invi said: he's just making baseless assumptions given the situation. There's no evidence to tie his accusations to anyone, let alone one of us."

"Maybe there's something he hasn't told us," Ava gently admonished—mostly because she didn't want to believe Ira's claims herself.

"Then he needs to tell us. How dare he look at us with suspicion. We're his comrades!" Aced snapped with genuine anger.

Gula simply shrugged. "I wouldn't call us 'comrades'…," he murmured. "Anyway, could you get to the point? I know you didn't call us here just to complain."

Gula wanted to cut to the chase and get this meeting over with as quickly as possible, which was why Aced didn't beat around the bush before laying out his proposal. "I want the three of us to form an alliance."

"But alliances are forbidden, Aced!" Ava immediately refused.

"I knew it. I had a feeling it might come to this. So we join forces, then confront Ira?" Gula seemed a bit exasperated, but he knew where Aced was coming from.

"Confronting him is pointless. Ira won't change his mind."

Aced was normally so blunt, but here he was being just a tad equivocal. It made his two comrades wonder if he didn't actually suspect Ira at all.

Meanwhile, Aced kept laying his cards on the table. "I know there's darkness at work. There's no question. But I don't believe for a second there's a traitor among us. Unfortunately, Ira doesn't share the same belief. He's just wasting time trying to figure out who the traitor is. But darkness won't wait, and neither should we. We need to band together now and find a way to fight it."

"Guess it makes sense," said Gula, impressed by Aced's fluid presentation of his idea.

"I agree that we need to do something to fight the darkness, but combining our Unions? That was strictly forbidden by the Master."

It seemed Ava was still just as unsure of what to do as she was at the meeting the other day.

"He's no longer here," Aced said quietly, his eyes drifting away. The

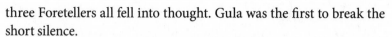

three Foretellers all fell into thought. Gula was the first to break the short silence.

"I'm in. But let's be clear: the alliance is just between the two of us right now. I don't want my Union members involved."

"Gula!"

Ava raised her head to look at her fellow apprentice, who had just chosen to go against the teachings of their Master. Ava looked away once she realized Aced was watching her, then said, "I want… I want to follow the Master's teachings."

Aced's reply was unexpectedly kind. "Understood. That's your choice to make. You should do whatever you feel is right."

"Yeah." Ava nodded with relief, and her gaze drifted downward again.

But Gula still had questions. "By the way, Aced, do Ira and Invi know?"

"I haven't talked to Ira about it for obvious reasons, but I did ask Invi to join us," said Aced. His eyes moved to the entrance of the warehouse—just as Invi herself arrived.

"You wanted to see me?"

She stopped short as she noticed the younger two.

"Gula, Ava, what're you doing here? What's the meaning of this?"

Gula gave an easy wave of the hand, while Ava kept her eyes lowered.

"Hear me out, Invi. I want an alliance among our Unions. Gula here has already agreed. Will you join us and together we can—"

"And disobey the Master's teachings?!"

Invi cut off Aced's entreaty harshly, but he didn't give up.

"We don't have a choice! Darkness is approaching, and we need to combine our strength to stand against it."

"The Master bestowed each of us with a different role, and he specifically told us to keep our Unions separate to maintain the balance of power. He told us any imbalance would lead to a desire for more power, which leads to darkness. I know you haven't forgotten! Perhaps…it's you who has been tainted by darkness."

Tainted by darkness…

The Foreteller in the bear mask trembled in anger at such an accusation.

"I'm tainted by darkness? Then what about you, Invi? You spy on us and report everything you see back to Ira! You really think you have no darkness in your heart after what you did?!"

"Because that is my role," Invi replied coolly to her furious comrade.

"To observe us, yes. But not to disclose everything we say and do to Ira!"

Invi averted her gaze at Aced's fierce reproach. And he still wasn't done.

"For all we know, you and Ira could be allies, scheming behind our backs!"

"That's enough."

Ava watched their angry exchange uneasily.

Now it was evening.

Ava was in the square alone, sitting on the edge of the fountain and gazing absentmindedly at the sky.

"When will it stop? I don't want us to turn against each other…," she whispered.

Just then a lone Keyblade wielder approached—Ephemer, the boy with silver hair.

"Master Ava!" he called. The two of them had met before.

"Oh. Hello! Your name is Ephemer, right?"

"Uh-huh! Uh, hey, can I join you?"

"Uh-huh," Ava replied, and then Ephemer sat down next to her.

"Why the long face? Did something happen?" he asked straightaway.

"Long day… Do you remember what you asked me before? About

why the Unions compete against each other instead of working together? Actually, I always wondered the same thing."

"Huh? Isn't it just because the Master said so?" Ephemer asked, confused.

"Yes, and as such we must obey. The Master said so, so it is. But lately, I've really started to wonder. You once told me that you were looking for answers, that you wanted to solve the mysteries of this world. Well, I think that's how things should be. We need to question things and think for ourselves."

Ephemer shrugged. Was that how she really felt? "Whoa! You're really not yourself today. I guess even Foretellers have their off days. Hey, maybe talking about the Book will cheer you up!" he offered cheerily.

Ava's mood improved a little, too. "Not a chance!" she said with a smile.

"Awww," Ephemer complained with exaggerated petulance.

"You were trying to pull a fast one on me, weren't you?" she scolded good-naturedly, like a teacher to a misbehaving student.

"No, no, I was joking!"

"If you say so." Ava stood, and the conversation could have ended there. But then she seemed to have second thoughts. "But, to be honest, I think it would be great if all the Unions could work together and be friends."

Ephemer perked up and hopped down from the lip of the fountain.

"You know, I made a friend from another Union today. Wasn't much of a talker, maybe just shy. We're meeting again tomorrow."

"That sounds like so much fun! Then, you'd better go home and get some sleep."

"'Kay!" he replied enthusiastically before telling her earnestly, "Well, it was nice talking to you. I don't know what's got you down, but please cheer up!"

With a proper bow, Ephemer then hurried off on his way.

"Thank you," Ava murmured as she watched him go. "If the worst

happens, I'll be glad to leave the future to the kids who see the world in the way that you do."

With this resolution in her heart, Ava looked up at the sky. A single fuzzy dandelion seed danced in the air, brought to her by the breeze.

"Let the wind carry you far, far away...my Dandelions."

The sun set over Daybreak Town.

Aced was alone in the Master's chamber, waiting for the Master himself. It was completely silent, except for the turning gears.

"You been here long?" the Master called when he finally returned. "My bad."

"No." It was easy to tell Aced was nervous, even with the bear mask covering his face.

"So, what did you want?" The Master sat down in his chair and looked up expectantly at Aced.

"You didn't forget, did you? You're the one who called me here," the Foreteller replied, startled.

"Lighten up, I was just kidding! I didn't forget. Give me a little credit here. I was just testing you!" The Master loved his jokes, but Aced was just confused.

"R-right..."

"Now then, allow me to tell you about your role. You're going to be Ira's right-hand man."

"What? Ira's right-hand man? What do you mean?"

That sounded awfully big for such an offhand announcement; now Aced was even more bewildered. Either way, it was evident the bear-masked Foreteller didn't think much of the idea.

"Well, Ira's gonna be the new leader after I'm gone, you see, so just stand by him," explained the Master, who then turned to his desk and opened the Book of Prophecies, indicating that there was nothing left to be said. "Don't disappoint."

"Explain to me, Master. What do you mean Ira's going to be the leader?" Aced persisted, perhaps dissatisfied with his assigned task. The Master turned to face his pupil.

"What? Is that disappointment I hear? Did *you* want to be the leader?"

Aced snapped to attention. "No!" he cried hurriedly. "I mean, if you had asked me to be the leader, that'd be a different story, but I wasn't trying—"

"You really wanna be leader, huh?" the Master of Masters teasingly remarked.

"I, well…"

"I know you want it, but that just isn't enough. Any chump can say, 'You! Here's a huge promotion. Good job!' and make you head honcho, but enthusiasm alone doesn't make a great leader. Ira needs someone like you to give him a push in the right direction," explained the Master readily.

"I agree; Ira is definitely the most worthy among us. I'm sure he'll make a fine leader."

"Then it's settled."

Though the Master turned away, suggesting the conversation was at an end, Aced just couldn't let the issue go.

"Wait, I agreed that he is worthy. But why do we *need* a new leader, Master? Does—does that mean you will no longer be teaching us?"

The Master pondered the question for a moment, then slowly replied. "Well…I might disappear one day…"

Aced swallowed nervously.

"Well…I might disappear—," the Master repeated, hamming it up with a weak, melodramatic performance.

"Disappear?! Why? Where?!" Aced demanded.

"Speak up sooner if you're listening. That was embarrassing for me! Anyway, I don't know if I'm gonna disappear or not. It's anyone's guess right now." Sweeping his embarrassment under the rug, the Master quickly shifted back to the main topic.

Aced still wasn't satisfied. "But..."

"In any case, you need to support Ira," the Master continued, trying to mollify him. "We both know he's quite serious. He's always just thinking and thinking and thinking behind that unicorn mask of his, so everyone will be counting on you to spur him into action."

"Uh...right," Aced acquiesced, though he was still at a loss.

Slowly, the Master stood and put a hand on his student's shoulder. "You might not be entirely happy with your role, but just know that it's the most important one. Capisce?"

The hint of kindness in the Master's voice only confused Aced more.

"Shall I elaborate? Making Ira the leader is all good in theory, but sometime later you might think, 'Ooh, he's terrible at this,' in which case it'll be your job to step up. Who knows? Your leadership might be just what everyone needs. And that is your true role," the Master of Masters whispered into his student's ear.

At the end of his speech, he had one final, terribly important bit of advice.

"May your heart be your guiding key. Best of luck, Aced!"

Chapter 5

YOU WERE DREAMING AGAIN.

This time, you were in the Fountain Square, waiting for your friend to arrive.

"Sorry!"

Ephemer, the silver-haired boy who you thought wasn't going to show, came running up.

"I'm sorry. I really am! There was something important I had to take care of. I hope you can forgive me," he said, smiling as he placed his hands together and ducked his head apologetically. "Are you still up for our adventure?"

You accepted his invitation with a grin and a nod. Your destination was, of course, the underground waterway leading to the clocktower, which you hadn't been able to visit that day.

Though the two of you didn't speak much as you forged a path through the Heartless, the bond between you was plain to see.

You slipped between the houses along the steps up from the Fountain Square, then descended the stairs to the waterway and took the ladder down to the sewer. As before, the air there was chilly and damp. You pressed onward and reached the big gears right in front of the clocktower.

"It's up ahead. Are you with me?"

You looked up at the enormous interlocking wheels. Behind them were secrets to be discovered.

"Ah, you're not ready yet. I had a feeling that might be the case," he said behind you.

You turned to look at him.

"I'll be waiting," he said, and with those parting words, he vanished, leaving behind only a fuzzy dandelion seed floating off on the breeze amid a glimmering light. You just stood there in shock.

Ephemer would be waiting? But where?

"Did you have another dream?" I asked as you woke up.

Sitting up in bed, you hung your head in disappointment. It really was just a dream.

"It was about your friend, wasn't it?"

You nodded and told me about what you saw. Then you told me what you'd decided to do next.

"You want to go search for him in the tower? No way!"

You simply got out of bed and headed for the door.

"Only the Foretellers are allowed there. Besides…now's not a good time."

My point about the timing gave you some pause.

"I can't go into detail, but the Foretellers… Well, lately, they've been disagreeing on a few things. Let's just say you should steer clear of that tower for the time being."

Trouble between the Foretellers? You thought about it for a while—and maybe you thought Ephemer's disappearance was connected to it all.

You dashed from the room.

You headed for the front of the clocktower. I was standing right beside you, extremely worried.

"I don't think this is a good idea…," I said, but you continued to carefully search the area.

Just as you when you checked with Ephemer previously, there didn't appear to be a way in from the front.

"Are you even listening?"

You broke into a run.

"Wait! Where are you going?!"

I hurried after you. You were going to the place you saw Ephemer in your dream—the underground waterway, which was also where you last split up with him.

You were fighting through the swaths of Heartless when you encountered another Keyblade wielder, a boy with short hair and somewhat sharp eyes. He was busy thinning out the Heartless of Daybreak Town to gather Lux, much like you did.

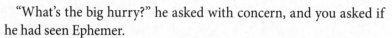

"What's the big hurry?" he asked with concern, and you asked if he had seen Ephemer.

"Ephemer? No, I don't know anyone by that name... But people have definitely been going missing."

That was true—you'd seen it yourself. Ephemer wasn't the first to break a promise to you.

"I may not know your friend, but I have seen people gathering in the square lately. Beats me what they're up to."

That was news to you. Elsewhere in Daybreak Town, things were changing. Maybe it had something to do with what I was telling you earlier, about the discord between the Foretellers.

You said good-bye to the Keyblade wielder and started back along the path from the waterway to the Fountain Square. On the stairs up from Waterfront Park, you encountered another wielder, a girl with pink hair and a kind face. You tried asking her about what the other boy had told you.

"I don't know anything about a meeting in the Fountain Square, but I have heard rumors that one of the Foretellers is assembling some of the best Keyblade wielders, even if they're from a different Union." More new intel. She continued, "I believe it's Master Ava, the one in the fox mask. These days, I see her around the square all the time..."

You tried asking her about Ephemer.

"What? A boy with silver hair? I think I saw him talking to Master Ava the other day."

Ava—you knew the Foreteller's name, but you had never spoken to her before.

You thanked the girl and then kept moving. What was making you so nervous? You hurriedly dispatched the packs of Heartless on your way back toward the sewer.

And awaiting you there was—

"Master Ava...?!" I exclaimed as I appeared beside you. The woman before us was the fox-masked Foreteller the girl had mentioned.

This was your first time meeting a Foreteller who wasn't Master

Invi. When you explained the rumors that had brought you here, Master Ava answered with a question of her own: "Why were you trying to find me?"

You replied honestly—that you were looking for Ephemer.

"Ephemer? Yes, I know him, but you still haven't answered my question," the Foreteller stated curiously. You filled her in on the details, including what you heard from the Keyblade wielders you met earlier. "You came to find me because of some rumor?" she said in slight disbelief.

That's when you told her about your dream from that morning.

"You had a dream? I see. Ephemer said he was waiting for you here in your dream, but this place is restricted. So you thought that he may have gotten caught up in the problems that we Foretellers have been having lately. And because someone saw us talking the other day, you thought that maybe I had something to do with it."

You nodded, and Master Ava smiled at you.

"You're honest. I like you. You're not too far off base, but I can't tell you much else right now," she said, then summoned her Keyblade to her hand.

"Master Ava?!" I yelped.

She pointed her Keyblade in your direction. "Show me what you can do."

With that, she sprang into action, swinging her Keyblade down toward you. You barely managed to summon your own Keyblade in time to block the blow.

"Very nice."

Master Ava was still smiling beneath her fox mask. You struggled mightily to push back her Keyblade, but she only hopped back lightly with a twirl of her robe as if it were nothing at all.

"Let's see how you handle this."

Then she brandished her Keyblade and fired off a barrage of glowing projectiles, which you desperately dodged as you moved out of range. They were coming down so thick that you didn't have a

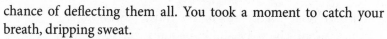

chance of deflecting them all. You took a moment to catch your breath, dripping sweat.

"Okay, now it's your turn."

You responded to Master Ava's challenge by charging at her head-on. Your Keyblades clashed together. While you were trying your hardest, Master Ava still had a grin on her face as she parried your attack and sent you crashing to the floor.

"Look out!" I cried.

Just when I thought all was lost, Master Ava's Keyblade vanished from her hand.

"Not bad. I see a lot of potential in you," she said before extending her hand. You took it and slowly got to your feet. "But I also see sadness in your heart. Hanging on to it will eventually lead to darkness. You need to somehow let it go."

Sadness? What kind of sadness was in your heart?

Next Master Ava looked over at me. "With this little one helping you, you'll be fine. Now, go home. And I'm sorry, but this area is strictly off-limits, all right?"

You got to your feet and bowed in response, realizing this was some sort of test. I followed your lead and bowed as well. I hurried over to you, and then we took our leave.

"So it's you. You're the friend he told me about...," Master Ava murmured once she was alone in the underground waterway.

It was night, and you were asleep.

"That was one doozy of a day. Betcha didn't think you'd end up having to fight a Foreteller," I said to you from the window.

Suddenly, the curtains rippled.

"I'm sorry. But it wasn't fun for me either, you know."

I spun toward the voice and leaped in surprise—Master Ava was sitting on the windowsill.

"Master Ava?! What are you doing here?"

"Please, call me 'Ava.'" She stood up and came over by me to watch you sleep for a moment. Then she returned her gaze to me. "Did you show him the dream of Ephemer?"

"No. That wasn't me." I shook my head.

Ava looked at you again. "Then perhaps it was Ephemer himself."

"Huh? How is that possible?"

I was puzzled over the idea, but then Ava quietly explained. "Ephemer's getting very close to the truth. He's fallen into an unchained state and now finds himself in a different realm. From that realm, I believe he tried reaching out to him," she said, placing a hand on your forehead. "If they connected, even in a dream, that means he's getting closer to that realm, too. Whether he continues down that path is up to his own heart."

Ava then removed her hand. It was as if she had cast some kind of spell.

"Chirithy, you have to protect them from the nightmares, so the wind can carry them far away from here."

Ava graced me with a smile, and then began to walk away, eventually vanishing as if she had been a dream herself.

Once she was gone, I snapped out of my daze and looked over at you. I got the feeling I knew the meaning of what she had said.

"Me...?"

As far as I knew, your sleep that night was dreamless.

—Right around then, Invi arrived back at the clocktower, where Ira was reading the Book of Prophecies.

"Invi? Have you learned something?" Ira asked as he turned the pages of the tome.

"It seems Aced and Gula's Unions are now allied."

Ira's hand paused at the report. "So Aced is the traitor after all," he declared, but Invi quickly rejected the notion.

"No, I don't believe he is."

Ira looked up at his fellow Foreteller. "Why's that?"

"To Aced, unification is a means of gathering strength to oppose the darkness. So I believe his heart still belongs to the light."

"Even so, forming alliances was strictly forbidden by the Master," Ira said sharply, placing a hand on the Book. He wasn't convinced by Invi's interpretation.

Her reply was firm as well. "Yes, and his teachings are absolute. That's why I will try and persuade Gula to dissolve their alliance."

"Then, I'll do it."

As Ira got to his feet, Invi stopped him. "No. Please, let me do the talking. Your intervention would do nothing more than spur Aced's anger."

Her calm resolve was enough for Ira. He returned to his seat and said, "All right. I'll leave it to you."

Invi nodded. "And one more thing," she said. "Aced has begun to question the two of us. As a precaution, my reports will be less frequent. I don't want him to get the wrong idea. Please understand."

"Yes, I do."

Once Ira was in agreement, Invi left. Ira turned back to the desk, reopened his Book of Prophecies, and began poring over it again.

And some time passed.

One day, Aced entered a warehouse in Daybreak Town with Gula close behind him.

"I think I'm done," the smaller Foreteller in the leopard mask murmured, half to himself.

Aced turned back. "Done with what?"

"The alliance. I think it's time to call it quits."

At that, the bear-masked Foreteller gave Gula a long look. "For what reason?"

"To put it simply, I entered this alliance thinking we were preparing to fight some impending darkness, but it hasn't come. In fact, there haven't been any suspicious incidents recently, and you haven't rallied anyone else to your cause."

Gula looked up at his much taller comrade. Aced's eyes darted this way and that, searching for something to say, and Gula sighed. It was hard to tell if he was disappointed with the current situation or with Aced himself.

"This alliance is meaningless. Even Invi agrees."

"Invi?!" Aced shouted.

Gula deflated a little. "Uh-oh, you weren't supposed to find out."

"Is Invi the one who told you to break our alliance?"

Despite Aced's mounting anger, Gula was still relatively relaxed.

"Maybe. But I'm the one who decided to do it, and I've already told you why."

"But we don't even know who the traitor is yet!"

Aced stepped forward, towering over Gula as he pressed his argument, but the smaller Foreteller was not to be swayed.

"And that's exactly why. I just can't trust anyone but myself."

"Don't you realize you won't stand a chance against the darkness on your own?" Aced cried furiously, but Gula was already turning away.

"Sorry, my mind's made up."

Without a second glance, he was gone.

Now alone, Aced clenched his fists.

"Invi, you will regret this!" he hissed with loathing.

You arrived before a large mansion in a new world, the Castle of Dreams, where Heartless were chasing something around the sprawling garden. Closer inspection revealed their quarry to be a brown mouse.

"Let's help him out!" I called, and you hurried after the Heartless and took them down.

After you had dealt with the last of the Heartless and paused to catch your breath, the little mouse came running up to you.

"You save Jaq! Thanks!" he squeaked with relief.

You replied with a gesture that said he was very welcome.

The mouse was about to run back to the mansion when he skidded to a halt, suddenly realizing something.

"Huh?!" He turned to face you. "You know what Jaq say?"

You nodded happily.

"Just like Cinderelly! I'm Jaq. Nice to meet ya."

You introduced yourself as well. Who was this "Cinderelly," though?

Jaq noticed my curiosity. "Cinderelly? She's our friend. She's nice, very nice," he explained. "I show you. This way!"

We accepted Jaq's invitation into the residence…except that we took the back entrance instead of the front door. We eventually came to an attic room at the top of some not-so-tidy steps.

Inside was a girl staring at a mannequin with a dress on it. She was beautiful, even in her rags.

"Oh. Hello, Jaq. I see you've brought a guest," the girl said. So this was Cinderelly.

"This is Jaq's friend. Good friend," the little mouse declared proudly.

"Why, that's wonderful. I'm Cinderella. It's a pleasure to meet you." Cinderella smiled brightly, then returned her attention to the dress. "There's going to be ball at the palace! And by royal command, every eligible maiden is to attend. But of course, I'll need something to wear."

In that dress, Cinderella would certainly be even lovelier than she was now.

But—

"Cinderella!" three women's voices called from downstairs.

Cinderella sighed. "All right, all right, I'm coming!" she replied, hurrying out of the room.

"Poor Cinderelly… She not go to the ball," Jaq said sadly after he watched her leave. "You'll see. They'll fix her. Work, work, work! She'll never get her dress done."

Jaq circled the dress and looked it over—until an idea came to him. "Say, I got an idea! We finish her dress for her! First, we need some trimmings!"

You nodded with a grin to let him know you were happy to help.

"But look out for Lucifer. Him a meanie, sneaky cat… Follow me!"

The first thing you needed to find was a necklace.

Apparently, Cinderella's stepmother Lady Tremaine had a nice one hidden away somewhere.

We snuck into her room only to find Heartless there waiting.

"So many monsters! Where they all come from?" Jaq exclaimed. You shook your head with chagrin and prepared for another fight.

Heartless were drawn to the darkness in people's hearts, so Lady Tremaine and her cruelty to Cinderella would've been the main source.

Funny, though… Haven't there been lots of Heartless in Daybreak Town recently, too? Does that mean something in our home is calling them there?

While I was mulling this over, you finished off the last of the Heartless, and Jaq snatched up the gorgeous string of pearls. "Let's get outta here!"

We left the room, but then—

"Whoa!"

Before us sat a large cat. Jaq dropped the necklace. "Oh no! Lucifer!"

The cat glared at you and growled before snatching up the necklace from the floor in his jaws and running off.

"Him a meanie cat, but us need pretty necklace for Cinderelly's dress! But all okay! Jaq got a new friend. Time to get necklace back!" Jaq cried bravely, and then the two of you went after the archnemesis of the mice. There were Heartless in the hallway as well, but you defeated them one by one and finally cornered the cat.

You cautiously edged closer to Lucifer, but then Heartless appeared around him. He leaped into the air in surprise, tail bristled, and dropped the necklace.

"Got it!"

Jaq came running over. Now all we had to do was get rid of those Heartless.

"You stay here?"

You replied with a glance, then turned to face them.

"Good! I'll go make Cinderelly's dress real pretty!" Jaq squeaked, then picked up the necklace and ran off.

"Oh well. What's a royal ball? After all, I supposed it would be frightfully dull...and boring...and completely...completely wonderful," Cinderella whispered to herself, climbing the last stairs to the attic. She had given up on the idea of going to the ball. She entered the dark room, closed the door with her back, and let out a long sigh.

Then Jaq lit a lamp.

"Oh, it's my...!"

The light revealed her dress, now completed.

"Surprise! It's you dress!" Jaq exclaimed reverently, bringing a smile to our faces.

I'm so glad we made it in time.

"I never dreamed— It's such a surprise!"

"Hurry, Cinderelly! Hurry! The ball!" Jaq sprang up to her shoulder, and Cinderella beamed at him.

"Oh, thank you so much!"

Now she would be able to go to the ball.

"I'm so glad," I said with true relief, while you watched Cinderella and Jaq celebrate.

A few months had passed since your encounter with Master Ava.

You had just returned to Daybreak Town after a mission to collect Lux and took a seat on the edge of the fountain. It was almost dusk. You had put in a good day's work.

"You did great out there, champ!" I said as I arrived. You looked a bit worn out. "I know it's a tough job, but someone's gotta do it... I know, I know. But if you give up now, the other Unions will get ahead."

The praise only seemed to dampen your spirits. There was no denying that Keyblade wielders had become more competitive when it came to dealing with the Heartless these days.

Just then, you heard a girl's voice. "But why does that matter?" You and I looked up to see a young woman with long, straight black hair coming this way. She had pretty eyes with long lashes, and she was evidently a Keybearer herself. "It's not a competition. Or at least it shouldn't be. Our goal of protecting the light is the same. There's no need for us to fight."

The black-haired girl stopped in front of you.

"Who're you?" I asked.

She sat down beside us, then smiled at you. "The name's Skuld, from Anguis." Same Union as you. She offered her hand in greeting. "Nice to meet you!"

You clasped her hand and shook it as you made your introductions. Her gaze was cool and even. "Ephemer told me all about you."

You and I shared a startled glance.

"Don't look so surprised! He used to be in my party, you know. We met not long after I became a Keyblade wielder. There was never a dull moment with him around! But then one day, he just quit."

It was easy to see why, since Ephemer was a part of a different Union, after all.

"I was really upset about it for a while… But then he showed up in my dream the other night and told me to find you!"

You and I looked at each other again.

"Why?" I asked, but Skuld just shrugged.

"Good question. I was actually hoping you could tell me. See, I don't really understand why he was in my dream to begin with." She smiled awkwardly, then added, "But he asked me to go with you. So here I am."

You told Skuld that you had dreamed about Ephemer yourself.

"He was in your dream, too? What'd he say?"

You explained the dream in detail, how Ephemer had told you that he would be waiting down in the underground waterway.

"Hmm…" Skuld crossed her arms in thought. "If he's waiting for you, then—" After a moment of contemplation, she looked up. "Why don't we go to the place you're supposed to meet him?"

You started to agree, so I had to step in.

"No way! Master Ava told us to stay away from there!"

"Well, there has to be a reason she said that. And I have a feeling it's the same reason Ephemer asked me to go with you. So let's get moving—"

Before she could finish her sentence, Skuld was interrupted by a tremendous noise that sounded like something big getting smashed, or maybe like two large objects crashing together.

"What was that?!" I jumped up in surprise.

"It came from nearby!"

You and Skuld looked in the direction where the racket had originated.

"Let's go!"

*   *   *

Skuld ran off toward the noise with you in tow.

"H-hey! Where're you going?!"

Flustered, I hurried after the two of you.

Aced was alone, catching his breath in a back alley of Daybreak Town.

It's been over a year since the Master left. It's time for me to fulfill my true role, he thought with his hand clenched against his chest. He burst out onto the main avenue with a downward swing of his Keyblade. The one he was attacking was Invi.

Aced's Keyblade whistled through the air toward her, but the serpent-masked Foreteller parried the blow. His next attack was a powerful swing through empty space, creating a cutting wave of force that surged toward Invi, but she lithely leaped away.

Their Keyblades clashed again as they fought.

"Why do you get in my way?" shouted Aced, already out of breath.

Invi was panting as well, but she quickly exhaled a single breath to regain her composure. "Don't be so conceited!" she cried. "I'm protecting the balance, just like the Master told us to! You need to come to your senses!"

Neither of them noticed Gula crouched in the shadow of a building, observing their confrontation.

"If we don't do something, the light will expire! Then we won't be able to avoid the grim future that awaits. We need to defy the Master's teaching to protect the world!" Aced bellowed.

It was true; the Book of Prophecies did foretell the defeat of the light.

"You're saying he was wrong?!"

"He's not here anymore. I won't let his prophecy come true. I won't let the world fall into darkness!"

He meant to save the worlds himself.

Above all else, Invi cared for fairness and justice. To her, this declaration was sheer arrogance, and she could not let it pass.

"You fool!" she exclaimed at last, while Gula rose to his feet in the shadows.

Aced must be the traitor...

Just then, Ava and someone's Chirithy came running into his field of view. Gula circled around to meet them so that the other two Foretellers wouldn't realize he had been watching.

"Ava, over here!" he yelled, joining her and rushing back over to where Aced and Invi faced off.

"Invi, Aced! What's going on?!" cried the Foreteller in the fox mask. She sounded pained.

"I found out who the traitor is, regrettably," Invi explained, her Keyblade still pointed at Aced.

"No, that's not true!" Ava looked about in confusion before focusing on Gula. He was ready to fight, too.

"Ava, there's no time to lose!" he urged.

Though hesitant, Ava called her own Keyblade, and she joined Invi and Gula against Aced.

"May my heart be my guiding key," he said in a voice perhaps too quiet for the other three to hear.

How had it come to this? How?

Was this truly the future that had been foreseen?

You came upon Master Invi, the leader of your Union, and Aced, the unfamiliar bear-masked Union Master, locked in combat.

Their struggle was fierce, so fierce that you realized how much Master Ava had been holding back during your battle with her.

"The Foretellers! Why are they fighting?" Skuld lamented, biting her lip in trepidation. "Ephemer was right...," she said softly, then looked over at you. "It's what I was trying to tell you earlier. Just before I woke up, he told me...the end of the world is near."

You and I both swallowed nervously.

"The end?!" I asked in alarm.

Skuld just nodded her head. "Yeah. After what we just saw, I can't help thinking it's true. The world will disappear, just like Ephemer did."

Your head lowered for a moment, but you quickly pulled yourself together. You beckoned for Skuld and me to follow you. "Let's go."

I could hear mournful determination in your voice.

"What?" I asked, startled, but Skuld simply nodded.

"Lead the way."

You started off with Skuld behind you.

"Wait, what? What just happened?"

I scurried after the two of you, still perplexed.

It seemed the Master of Masters hadn't noticed Gula enter.

"Master," he called, but his teacher was completely focused on the Book of Prophecies.

Gula quietly peeked over the Master's shoulder. "Um…Master? If you're busy, I can always come back later."

Finally noticing his pupil, the Master murmured, "Sure. Oh! No, no, no, stay! Now where— Ah, here it is!" He tore out a page of the Book and handed it to Gula as he got to his feet.

"What's this?"

"Go on, read it."

Gula skimmed the page the Master handed him—and then he realized something. "This is from the Book of Prophecies. But—"

"Yup. It's a page that's not in any of your Books."

This page had been removed from the copies of the Book that belonged to the other four Foretellers. And yes, it recorded events that none of them knew—except for Gula.

"And what's written here is…"

"Your role. You must find the traitor hidden among you and stop them before it's too late. And in order to help you find the traitor—"

Gula immediately deduced the Master's plan and raised his head. "I get it. That's why you gave us all different roles, isn't it?" he answered before the Master had even finished speaking. "If anyone deviates from the job they were given, we can easily conclude that they are the traitor. It's brilliant."

Despite Gula's praise, the Master turned away with a pout. "Way to steal my thunder, show-off!"

"Huh?"

Gula stared at the Master, puzzled.

"It's not fair. My plan was supposed to blow your mind with its grandeur. Your jaw should've hit the floor at my sheer genius!" the Master declared, dramatically pretending to get struck by lightning himself.

It still wasn't enough to faze Gula. "I'm...sorry? But was my logic flawed?"

"No, you're right. So, I guess now you've earned your time in the limelight," the Master replied with resignation, focusing on Gula again. His voice turned low and serious. "Even though there is a traitor, act normal and keep focused," he ordered. "Trust no one but yourself."

A little nervous, Gula nodded to show his understanding.

Chapter 6

AS YOU AND SKULD WERE RUNNING ALONG THE PATH from Waterfront Park to the tower, three dark figures with wings and eyes of dull gold suddenly materialized in front of you. They resembled Heartless, and yet their humanity wasn't entirely gone— they were an unknown, different sort of creature.

No... Are these...?

"...ux...Lux... Give...Lux...," the trio growled as they crept toward you.

"What are you?!" Skuld raised her Keyblade to defend herself. "What's going on?!"

One of the creatures croaked out a noise resembling an eerie laugh, and then all three of them sprang at once, screeching, "Give me Lux!" They fired bolts of magic at Skuld, but you burst into action and blocked them at the last moment.

"No way... I think these are...!" Skuld still couldn't decide what to do.

If these beings were calling for Lux, that could only mean one thing. But was that even possible?

You did your best to fend off their attacks, but when you prepared to go on the offensive...

"No!" Skuld stopped you.

"...Heya."

As the dark Chirithy sauntered up from behind the trio, they stepped back and ran off, leaving him to take care of the rest.

Meanwhile, I stepped in front of you and Skuld and faced my corrupted counterpart. This was my time to act, I knew.

"Aren't you...?"

"You don't look very happy to see me... Come on, I was just trying to help. I thought if I took away everyone's Lux, there'd be no reason to fight over it anymore. Aren't I the greatest?" said the black Chirithy, more to himself than to any of us here.

I shook my head sadly. "That color..."

"You like my new look?" he asked proudly.

"You've been tainted by darkness."

I was truly aggrieved. There was certainly no coming back for him now. That "new look" meant he had fallen.

"What's wrong?" he asked. "Do you hate darkness? Well, let me tell you a little secret: light and dark are two halves of the same coin. They're like day and night. One can't exist without the other. So you should embrace it like they did!"

I ignored him and pressed for answers instead. "You mean those three used to be human?"

"You betcha," the black Chirithy declared calmly.

Skuld's gaze dropped. "Were they wielders, too?" she asked, heartbroken.

"Right-o. But unlike you, those three can no longer use the power of the Book of Prophecies. The strength they fought you with was all their own! To be perfectly honest, they were pretty wimpy before. But darkness has a way of finding those with weak hearts and making them strong. Isn't darkness so sweet?"

"Those aren't the teachings!" I shouted before the dark Chirithy could say more. Every word out of his mouth was wrong.

"Teachings-smeechings! The truth of this world isn't something you can teach, Chirithy. It's something you have to learn for yourself."

I had another question for him, and this one was important. "Who is your wielder? Where are they?"

You and Skuld stared at the corrupted Chirithy. I don't know how many times he had showed up now, but every time his color was darker.

I was your Chirithy, but whose was he?

A knowing smirk appeared on his face. "Heh-heh-heh... Closer than you think."

He did a flip into the air and vanished, just like I always did.

"It can't be..." Skuld pressed her lips together and bowed her head.

"There's nothing we can do. They succumbed to darkness," I muttered in defeat, but her hands were clenched tight.

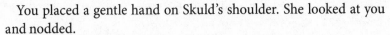

You placed a gentle hand on Skuld's shoulder. She looked at you and nodded.

"Yeah. You're right. We have to keep moving."

The two of you set off again.

There was virtually nothing to break the silence as you and Skuld proceeded through the underground waterway—just the quiet rush of water and turning gears. You were both probably preoccupied with thoughts of the three fallen wielders and the black Chirithy.

You and Skuld came to a halt.

"Is this where you last met with Ephemer?" she asked, turning to you.

You nodded quietly.

"There *has* to be something up ahead," she murmured.

I stared deeper into the blocked waterway, then moved to stand in front of you. "Are you sure this is a good idea? Between those three weirdos and that dark Chirithy, I don't have a good feeling about this."

I knew I had little chance of stopping you, but I still couldn't hide my worry. You gave me a gentle pat on the head, but you weren't turning back now.

"You know your way around the tower, don't you?" Skuld said, looking into my eyes.

"Y-yeah, why do you ask?"

"Well, I was hoping you could show us the way."

I instinctively looked over at you, and you nodded back at me.

"I—I suppose I could… But this area is off-limits, so once you get a quick peek, we're outta here. Okay?" I said emphatically.

You and Skuld shared a glance, and then she turned back to me. "Got it."

I let out a little sigh and walked into the clocktower.

After we climbed the stairs up and up and up, we reached the chamber of the Foretellers.

Skuld opened the door and peered around, and you stepped inside, too. You seemed slightly surprised; I'm sure you recognized it from your dream.

"What is this place?"

"This is the final room—the Foretellers' chamber," I replied. Skuld walked into the center of the room, which was surrounded by a mesh of gears instead of walls. The floor was scattered with piles of books and the tabletops with flasks and other scientific equipment.

"Do you think Ephemer was here?" wondered Skuld. I stepped up behind her to stop her from poking around the room any more than we had to.

"I don't know. But there's no one here now and nothing to see. Can we go now?"

My heart was pounding. We would be in *huge* trouble if someone caught us here, but I had no idea what the consequences would be.

"I guess. I was just expecting...more. It's kind of a letdown, really. I wonder what's so important about this place," Skuld said, turning to you. You crossed your arms in contemplation.

Both of you had dreamed about this place.

Who had shown them to you? The dark Chirithy, maybe?

"What are you doing here?" someone suddenly asked from behind.

"Master Invi!" I whispered. It was the snake-masked leader of your Union, Anguis.

"W-we're so sorry! We were just looking for someone," Skuld apologized. But if anyone was in trouble here, it was me.

"Chirithy, I expected more from you. You know that this area is off-limits."

"I-I'm sorry..." I followed Skuld's lead and bowed in apology.

"I caught another wielder in here just the other day. A friend of yours?"

"Yes, he is," you replied.

I looked over, surprised that you had spoken up so directly. You almost never talked.

Skuld was startled, too. "So he *was* here. Did you talk to him?" she asked Master Invi.

"Yes. But you must know that his Union gathers Lux for a reason that contradicts ours. He befriended you to get his hands on information, nothing more. But he is a threat no longer."

You gasped.

"Did you—? Is Ephemer—?" Skuld started to say, but Master Invi cut her off.

"He's gone."

In an instant, the air seemed to freeze over. I murmured your name, but you remained motionless.

Skuld was trembling. "How could you?!"

"What are you going to do?" Master Invi asked, prompting Skuld to summon her Keyblade.

"Nothing!" I frantically tried to stop her.

Strong as you may have been, the two of you were no match for a Foreteller. Challenging one of them would doom you to Ephemer's fate.

And yet Skuld stood stock-still, her Keyblade still directed toward Master Invi.

"Master Invi, this is my fault! All of it! They didn't do anything wrong," I pleaded desperately. I never should have brought the two of you here.

A gentle hand landed on my head—yours.

You quietly stepped in front of the Foreteller. "This whole thing was my idea," you said. "I was the one who wanted to look for Ephemer, and for good reason. You see, I've gone to different worlds to gather Lux; a lot of effort has gone into the contributions to my Union."

It was the first time I had ever heard you speak this much.

"I've even had to fight those I consider my friends. I've done everything that was expected of me without a second thought," you continued, while Skuld and I watched in shock. "And then I met Ephemer. We didn't know each other very long, but he left a lasting impression. Not all of our memories are good ones; in fact, he even broke one of our promises."

I remembered how sad you were back then, when Ephemer hadn't showed.

"No matter what happened, I knew we were still friends." You were looking at me as you said it. You had called me your friend, too.

You then calmly summoned your Keyblade to your hand.

"But you took him away from me. I feel sad, I feel angry, I feel hurt. Maybe that means I have darkness in my heart; I don't care."

You turned your Keyblade toward Master Invi, ready for a battle.

"But I can't let you get away with what you did to my friend. Even if I have to fight you, even if I don't stand a chance, even if I may disappear... I will, because I know in my heart that Ephemer would do the same if he were here. Master Invi, I mean no disrespect, but this is something I must do."

Master Invi called forth her own Keyblade and quietly shifted into a battle-ready stance. "So be it."

"No!" I cried, but I couldn't stop this.

You immediately leaped into the air for an overhead strike, but Master Invi blocked it. As Skuld struck out with her own Keyblade, the Master knocked both of you away. Skuld managed to land upright, but you went sprawling beside her. You quickly scrambled to your feet, though, and readied your Keyblade again.

The two of you didn't stand a chance against a Foreteller—Master Invi wasn't even using both hands. It was like she was testing you—which reminded me of something. Master Ava had also been less than serious when you two fought.

What if...?

I was powerless to do anything but watch, though.

Master Invi held her Keyblade out and fired off a magical light, which you were able to deflect. But it was the first of many, aimed at both you and Skuld.

Skuld shouted your name and charged in between you and the Foreteller. While she countered the magic with her Keyblade, you used the opening to rush in for an attack. Your Keyblade just barely grazed Invi, but hers landed a direct hit on your head. You collapsed.

I was beginning to fear the worst when a light filled the area.

The next thing I knew, we were in the underground waterway from before instead of in the Foretellers' chamber.

Skuld and I knelt and watched you anxiously where you lay. Luckily, it didn't look like you were injured too badly.

Your eyes fluttered open.

"Congratulations. You fought admirably," Master Invi said gently, and then light engulfed her as she transformed.

"Master Ava…?" Skuld exclaimed. It was indeed the Foreteller in the fox mask.

Ava walked over to you and held out her hand, sending a wave of warm light over you that healed you until you could stand again.

"Thank you for showing me the strength of your hearts. I hope you'll forgive me for deceiving you, but the Foreteller you fought, the room you were in, were both merely projections."

"But why? What was the point?" Skuld asked.

"It's as Ephemer stated in your dream," Ava told us solemnly, though none of us wanted to believe it. "The world will soon end."

Foretellers fighting each other, vanishing Keyblade wielders, and Ephemer, gone—all of it must have had something to do with the end of the world.

"But if all wielders disappear along with it, there will be no one left to drive away the ensuing darkness. So we must prevent this at all costs." Master Ava paced slowly as she explained, then came to a stop. "My role in all this is to gather wielders with great potential, regardless of their Unions. They must survive for the world after."

"The world after…?" I asked. I'd never heard about any of this.

"This is all so… I—I don't understand." It was a lot to take in; no wonder Skuld wasn't sure what to say.

I imagine you weren't, either; you just nodded in agreement.

"So what happened to Ephemer?" Skuld was cutting right to the chase: your friend's disappearance.

"Ephemer must've caught wind of the fact that there was more to everything than what he'd been taught, so he started questioning things. He went looking for the truth because he knew there was one to be found. That's how I knew he was the one." Ava turned to look at us. "The one I could count on to lead the Dandelions in my stead."

"Dandelions?"

I hadn't heard anything about this.

"They're a special group of Keyblade wielders that will remain after the rest of us are gone. It was my role to put the Dandelions together. But I have to be there when the inevitable events unfold, so I need someone to replace me when I'm gone. And I chose Ephemer. He accepted, and now he's far away from here, waiting."

"So then…he's all right?" Skuld asked hopefully.

Master Ava nodded in reply. "Yes, he's fine. However, this world is not. There is a wielder who has been corrupted, and the Chirithy you saw earlier is proof of that." She walked over to us slowly. "But I want the world to come to be filled with light. That's why only wielders with a strong resistance to darkness are chosen as Dandelions. So I ask both of you: Will you join us?"

You and Skuld looked at each other.

You lowered your head, while Skuld gave Master Ava a long look.

"Of course, Master Ava. Thank you," Skuld replied, but you didn't seem so sure. I watched you, worried. I would remain by your side no matter how you chose to answer, but—

"What's wrong?" Skuld asked.

You raised your head again. "What'll happen to the others? The ones who aren't chosen?" you asked Master Ava.

Her gaze drifted downward for a moment, then she looked up and said, "They will have no choice but to fight in the Keyblade War."

"The Keyblade War...?" Skuld whispered.

"I'm afraid it's inevitable," Ava finished sadly.

Everyone was silent for a time, until you looked at the Master again. "May I take some time to think about my decision?"

Your tone was firm. Skuld and I were surprised, but you remained resolute.

"Of course, take all the time you need. This decision is yours to make, and you should do what feels right. I just ask that you keep this to yourselves. I'm afraid the future is a very...sensitive subject."

After we nodded in understanding, Master Ava turned away and left.

Once we were back in the square, we sat on the rim of the fountain and looked up at the sky.

"What's holding you back from joining the Dandelions?" I asked you, even though I had some idea of your reasons. "You'd get to see Ephemer again!"

"Ephemer's my friend, and he's important to me. But so is everyone else, and I can't just abandon them."

"I understand." I was a little relieved to hear that answer, honestly; it showed me that you were still the same you. Well, except for how much you were talking all of a sudden.

Then it was Skuld's turn. "Can I share a story?"

You nodded.

"When I became a Keyblade wielder, I was so excited. I even made my own party, but no one wanted to join it. Finally, after what seemed like ages, Ephemer did," she said, fondly recounting her time with Ephemer. "For a long time, it was just the two of us. But as time passed, others joined us, and we spent all our time gathering as much Lux as possible. With our busy schedule, Ephemer and I spoke less and less, until one day he turned to me and said, 'Skuld, you'll be all right on your own now.' And then he left. I continued to collect Lux with my party members, but I guess people started to lose interest. One by one they left, until one day, it was just me again. And you know what? Ephemer was right. I *was* fine on my own. I never forgot about him, though."

I wondered what had happened to Skuld during that time.

Gathering Lux is an important mission for Keybearers, but you're free to do it however you want—with your Union, with your party, or even alone if you can't get along. There are some people out there who don't pull their weight. Everyone's different, which sometimes leads to arguments and party breakups.

"And I know he never forgot about me either, because he led me to you. You helped me see so much. Thank you. Now I just have to thank Ephemer, and the only way to do that is to join the Dandelions," Skuld said, then smiled at you. She hopped down from the edge of the fountain and turned your way. "Thanks. For everything."

She held her hand out to you, and you got down off the fountain and took it.

There was no doubt in my mind that the two of you would see each other again. You would always be friends no matter how far apart you were.

You would see each other again one day.

The Master of Masters stood facing the Foreteller Ava.

"What's written in the last page of the Book is gonna happen," the Master finally said, breaking the silence between them. "The entire world will be lost to darkness."

Ava closed her eyes. "But Master, isn't there anything we can do?" she asked, her voice full of frustration.

"Well, that's what brings me to your role," he replied. "You might just be the only hope of keeping the light from expiring."

Ava looked up and watched the Master intently. "Hope? Master, what is it that you need me to do?"

"Don't get involved in any battles, forget the notion of Unions, find Keyblade wielders with potential, and create an entirely separate organization. Then, like the seeds of a dandelion, let them fly to another world. They will keep the light alive." His voice was soft and earnest—he never spoke like this to the other Foretellers.

"You really think that...I'm the right person for this?"

"Ava, you're the only person for this," he gently admonished her.

Ava looked down for a moment but then quickly raised her head again. "I understand."

The Master nodded quietly at her decision.

Chapter 7

GULA, THE YOUNG FORETELLER IN THE LEOPARD MASK, was studying a piece of paper in an alley of Daybreak Town. Once again, he read over the words on the page—words meant for him alone among the Foretellers.

"Trust no one but myself," he murmured, then put the page in his robe and slowly walked away.

He was headed for the warehouse where Aced was hiding, injured from his battle with Invi, Ava, and Gula.

When he arrived, the Foreteller in the bear mask was still breathing heavily. "Gula...," Aced gasped, spotting his fellow Foreteller.

"Do you wanna know what my role is?" Gula asked, standing over Aced.

The Foreteller returned the look with suspicion, wondering why he would be asking this now.

"The Books we were given are incomplete. There's a Lost Page."

"Lost Page?" This was news to Aced.

Gula continued: "On that page, it was written that there is a traitor." He summoned his Keyblade to his hand. "The Master told me...to find and stop that person."

Aced slowly struggled to his feet and clenched his fist. "I called you my comrade. But never again, Gula. It doesn't matter to me if you think I am the traitor and you want to strike me down. You knew there was a traitor, and you just watched silently as we fought each other, and I won't forgive you for that." Aced readied his own Keyblade.

"You can barely stay on your feet! Just give up already!" Gula shouted.

"Don't you underestimate me!" Aced yelled at the same time, and his Keyblade met Gula's.

Though he was wounded, Aced had quite a size advantage, to say nothing of his overwhelmingly superior strength and stamina. On the other hand, he couldn't hold a candle to Gula when it came to speedy swordplay. They would have been on equal footing if Aced were uninjured, perhaps—at least, if the bear-masked Foreteller hadn't had the greater wealth of experience to draw upon. That was why Gula had chosen to challenge him when he wasn't at a hundred percent. There was one flaw in his plan, though: The rage that drove Aced gave him strength that upset the balance.

Their Keyblades clashed again and again, giving off sprays of sparks each time. The two Foretellers jumped back and glared at each other across the distance. It seemed like their duel would last forever—but then Gula was the first to fall. Aced limped over to Gula, who had one knee on the stone, and raised his Keyblade to deliver a final, furious blow—when someone came running toward him.

"Please stop!" Ava leaped in front of Gula, shielding him, and Aced's Keyblade came to a halt. The Foreteller in the fox mask gazed at him, unflinching. Eventually, Aced lowered his arm and sent his Keyblade away.

"You too, huh?" he muttered sadly, then turned his back on the two Foretellers and stumbled off, dragging one leg behind him.

Ava hugged Gula. "Why?" she said in a small voice. "Why did it have to come to this?"

Aced limped down a backstreet of Daybreak Town, wounded in both heart and body.

Ira, the Foreteller in the unicorn mask, stood waiting for him.

"Come to finish me off? Then make it quick." Aced smirked bitterly.

Ira admonished him quietly. "That's not what brought me here today. I wish to fulfill the role bestowed upon me, that's all," he said. "It isn't our place to try and change the events of the future; that is not our mission. We're here to make sure that light lives on. With only five lights, we can't afford to lose any."

Five lights...? Aced wondered. "You...still count me as one of the five lights?"

"Of course."

Aced let out a small breath, perhaps slightly relieved by that response. "Only you could be such a good guy after everything we've been through. But hey, I guess that's one of the reasons I respect you so much." The anger in Aced's voice had been replaced by something akin to warmth—for a fleeting moment, at least. "However, we still might only be four."

Ira flinched slightly.

"I'm talking about Gula. He's using the knowledge of something called the Lost Page. He said that it contains events that are missing from all of our Books. He's using it to discover and apprehend whoever is the traitor, claims that's his role. But who knows what his real intentions are? What I do know is that I will never forgive him for hiding the fact that he knew someone would betray us. That's the biggest betrayal of all." The anger was creeping back into Aced's voice.

"I'd like to believe that Gula was simply carrying out his role… Aced, I'll deal with this matter. Please keep it to yourself for now," Ira advised him, turning to leave.

"Understood," Aced replied.

However, Ira was troubled as he walked on by himself. To think that the traitor he had foreseen actually existed.

…He had to get ahold of that Lost Page.

Ava brought the injured Gula beneath a bridge in Daybreak Town, all the way to the dead end in the underground waterway flowing into the clocktower. Gula should be able to recuperate here without being discovered.

"Someone's coming! They're headed straight this way!"

The first Chirithy created by the Master of Masters came running; he was Ava's companion now.

"Thanks, Chirithy. Take care of him," the Foreteller said, then climbed to the top of the bridge in front of the tower and found Ava approaching from the other side. She ran over to him, hoping to put a little more distance between him and Gula.

"Ira? Is something wrong?"

She flinched as his steely gaze turned on her. "I know Gula's here," he said.

"What?!" she gasped without thinking. How could he have known?

The unicorn-masked Foreteller didn't relent. "Tell me where he is."

"But why? What are you going to do?"

"None of your concern."

Ava was at a loss. Ira was their leader, and this was most likely an order. Still…

"Don't," she refused in a small voice.

"What?" Ira said.

Ava raised her head and faced Ira with determination in her eyes. "I won't let you near him."

"So that's it…," he murmured to himself, suggesting that he understood the situation. "All right. I'll go."

Ira turned on his heel and took his leave. Ava let out a sigh of relief as she watched him go, then ran back underneath the bridge where Gula was resting—or should have been.

"Gula, what are you doing?!"

The young Foreteller was trying to get up. Ava hurried over to him to offer support, but Gula brushed away her hands and sat up on his own. "Something happen?" he asked.

"Ira was here. He wanted me to give you up," she replied.

Gula's lips quirked into a little smile. "I knew it. It's finally come to this."

"Come to what?" Ava asked, completely in the dark.

Gula leaned back against the wall. "Everyone wants to know about the Lost Page."

The Lost Page had them all curious, and Ira had even come looking for Gula to learn more, but Ava hadn't heard of it.

"The Lost Page?"

"Yeah." Gula nodded, then began to elaborate. "It's a page the Master gave me. It doesn't exist in any of our Books. It contains a passage about an inevitable betrayal. It talks about 'the one who bears the sigil.' That's it. So I don't know what to make of it, to be honest. My role is to find out who it is. I suspected Aced and went to confront him. And look what happened." A frustrated smirk appeared on Gula's face.

"Why are you telling me this, Gula?" Ava asked. "I have enough to think about keeping with the Master's teachings and my role."

"Always walking the straight and narrow," Gula said, impressed. "I'm a fool for basing my actions on what is written on that Lost Page. Everything in the passage is ambiguous at best."

Gula had revealed slightly more than he meant to about the contents of the mysterious page—maybe it was because Ava was so trustworthy, he thought as he gave her a long look. "That's why I need to find out."

He gripped Ava's hand in his.

"But how?" she asked.

"By asking the Master."

"But he's not here anymore."

"I'm going to summon Kingdom Hearts."

"What?!" Ava was shocked to hear what he was planning.

"Then he'll have no choice but to come back," he stated in no uncertain terms.

"Summoning Kingdom Hearts is forbidden!"

"That's exactly why!" he exclaimed while holding Ava's right hand in both of his own, perhaps to assure himself of his own conviction. "The only way to get him back is to break the rules! If things don't change, the entire world is doomed! But in order to go through with it, I'll need Lux. I don't have nearly enough!" Gula tightened his grip on Ava's hand and looked her in the eye. "You always do the right thing. Help me with this."

…A short time passed, and Ava eventually averted her eyes from Gula's straightforward gaze.

"I'm sorry. I know you want the Master to return, but you don't know how summoning Kingdom Hearts will affect the rest of the world. The Master...he forbade it for a reason."

Ava broke off for a moment, removed Gula's hands from hers, then looked him in the eye again. "I'm afraid I can't help you," she said.

"I see."

He drew back from Ava, slowly got to his feet, and began to walk away.

"May your heart be your guiding key," he told her as he left. He didn't look back.

A few days later, Ava stood facing Invi on the bridge in front of the clocktower.

"Why did you tell Ira? It had to be you because you were the only one who knew where we were hiding. Didn't you think for a second that your actions could make things worse than they already are?" Ava implored.

Invi seemed a little less composed than normal in the face of Ava's accusations. "And why should that even bother you?" she fired back. "Not only do you have your Union, but you've also gathered the finest Keyblade wielders from other Unions, and you're training them in another location, aren't you?"

Ava wasn't about to let Invi misunderstand her mission. "Yes, because that is my role!"

That was the first time Invi had heard of this. For a moment, the Foreteller in the snake mask struggled to find a reply. "I had no idea...," she said at last with some regret. "I'm sorry. I overstepped."

"No. I shouldn't have snapped at you either," Ava said, calming down. She'd let her emotions get the better of her, too.

A silence passed between them, and it was Invi who finally broke it. "What did Ira want?"

"I don't know exactly." Ava shook her head, then continued

uncertainly. "He just asked me to give up Gula. His eyes... They were...scary. I was worried he'd do something awful. I knew I couldn't tell him where Gula was. Then he turned around and walked away."

Invi contemplated the news for moment. "I see. And Gula? How is he doing?"

Ava's eyes drifted away from the concerned Foreteller momentarily, then focused on a point below the bridge.

"I don't know. He's gone. Gula's on a mission to collect Lux," she said with sadness. Invi thought about this new revelation for a second as the pieces came together for her. "Ah. That explains why Aced and Ira are as well. They're trying to maintain the balance. But that isn't the balance we were expected to keep. If everyone's collecting light solely for themselves, Keyblade wielders will soon turn against one another, which will lead to..."

Invi paused, hesitant to say aloud the conclusion she refused to accept.

"...the Keyblade War."

Ava closed her eyes, too, then. She knew what came after that. "Then what's written in the Book, all of it will happen..."

Her voice trailed off, and in her stead, Invi followed this thread to its conclusion—the one recorded in the Book of Prophecies.

"Light will expire."

For a little while, the two didn't know what to say...

Is there truly no way to avoid this outcome?

"Invi, what are you going to do?" Ava asked as the other Foreteller began to walk away.

"I'll gather Lux, too," Invi replied. "No matter what, the balance must be kept. Ava, you do the same. We must...delay the inevitable." Without waiting to hear Ava's reply, Invi left.

"Right...," Ava murmured, in a voice almost too small to hear.

Maybe a day is coming when darkness covers the world, but I will keep the thread of hope alive.

*   *   *

In the Fountain Square, Ava stood before her handpicked Keyblade Wielders.

"Today you're here to continue with your training for our mission. This session may seem like it's familiar to you, but in a world that is different, one made of dreams…"

At this point in her speech, the Foreteller faltered, and a short wave of confusion passed among her audience of wielders.

"You are our hope," she said to them. "A war will soon wage. Those who strive to protect the light will turn their weapons on their allies for the sake of loyalty to their own Unions. To be honest, I don't know how far I can guide all of you. What you must remember is that anyone can lose themselves to the darkness."

After all, that darkness, those emotions, lurked in everyone's hearts. And that darkness would lead to the Keyblade War.

Was there really no way to stop it? Was the future truly inevitable?

"However, there will no winners: everything will be lost. Except all of you who are the seeds of hope. When the time comes, and there is war, you mustn't fight but instead you must fly away from here to the world outside. This training is to help you fulfill this crucial task. Their future is in all your hands—as is the world's light. May your heart be your guiding key."

I don't know anymore.

For the rest…I'll let my heart guide me.

Chapter 8

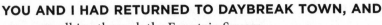

YOU AND I HAD RETURNED TO DAYBREAK TOWN, AND we were walking through the Fountain Square.

It was almost dusk.

After collecting so much Lux today, I'm sure you were exhausted. But it wasn't long before we heard other Keyblade wielders arguing.

"Not again…," I muttered. Such quarrels had become an all-too-common sight around town these days. You raised your head and started toward them; I could tell you wanted to break up the fight. That was just who you were.

But—

"Don't get involved. I know it's frustrating, but you can't fix everything," I said, grabbing the hem of your shirt.

You sighed, and your head drooped. "Everyone seems to have a bone to pick. I hope things don't get any worse."

Suddenly, the two wielders summoned their respective Keyblades. You dashed over to them, jumped between them, and blocked both weapons just in the nick of time.

"Wait! We're all on the same side!" I shouted as I hustled over, too.

One of them snorted at the idea, apparently ready to fight you next if he had to. He was wearing glasses and some frilly clothing. "Are we? Then why did they steal our Lux?"

The other wielder, who was wearing rabbit ears and a fluffy bunny costume, shot back, "What are you talking about? We're just trying to protect the light. I'll bet good munny that it's your Union that's fallen into darkness. Traitors!"

Despite the harsh words, both of them finally lowered their Keyblades—but they were still ready to fight again if they had to.

"What did you say?! How can you prove *you're* not the traitor?!"

Caught in the middle of their heated exchange, you spread your arms in an effort to prevent things from escalating.

"Hold on! We're all on the same side!" I called, doing my best to calm them down, too. "Why are you fighting?!"

Unfortunately, they weren't in the mood to listen.

"Mind your own business!" The wielder in the glasses raised his Keyblade, ready to strike.

"Stop it!" someone shouted.

Thank goodness! I thought we were completely on our own here!

The one coming to our rescue was Skuld.

The two Keyblade wielders gave her a dubious look.

"Who are you? Which Union do you belong to?" asked the wielder dressed like a bunny. Did no one trust people outside their own Union anymore?

"It doesn't matter. Our only enemy is darkness. Our Keyblades aren't meant to harm one another!"

What Skuld was saying was absolutely correct: Keyblades were for eradicating darkness.

The bunny wielder didn't agree. "Anyone trying to steal the light is no better than a dark monster themselves!"

"What?!" Skuld cried. Almost on cue, other Keyblade wielders arrived, drawn to the commotion. They were furious with Skuld, even though she was the one reminding them of the truth.

Oh, why is this happening…?

"The war's already begun," said the bespectacled wielder, and Skuld faltered for a moment.

"That's right," one of the newcomers asserted, adding more fuel to the fire. It was Master Aced, the Foreteller in the bear mask. "We can only place trust in our own Unions. We cannot tell who has fallen into darkness with a mere glance. Why do you fight over Lux? Light is not proof of strength. Victory is proof of strength. And a strong Union is proof of justice."

"What?" Skuld shouted. I could hear her grief.

Master Aced would not be dissuaded. "Do you disagree? Aren't you one of Ava's chosen wielders? One of the Dandelions? You, of all people, should be able to see that she's using her special Union to demonstrate her power."

Disheartened, Skuld's gaze drifted downward—and you stepped forward to face the Master in her place.

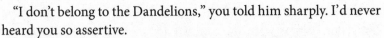

"I don't belong to the Dandelions," you told him sharply. I'd never heard you so assertive.

Aced looked over at you. "What Union do you belong to?"

"Anguis," you answered, and the Foreteller scoffed.

"Stand ready," he said with heavy finality, and a Keyblade appeared in his hand.

You didn't want to fight, but Master Aced didn't care. He only closed in to take the first strike himself.

"You can't do this!" I cried, but Master Aced had already made his choice. He closed the distance between you in a heartbeat and lashed out with his Keyblade. It was all you could do to stop the blow from reaching you.

It was hopeless, I knew… You were a goner.

You managed to buy yourself some space with a counterattack, then stepped forward and used the momentum to power an upward slash that grazed Aced's mask. Barely, just barely.

Unfortunately, your advantage only lasted for a moment, and the Foreteller quickly brought down his Keyblade on you with terrifying power.

You tried to block, but the force of his blow still sent you to your knees.

"You are unworthy of the Keyblade." He glowered down at you.

What should I do? What can I do?

"Enough, Aced. Put away your Keyblade." A reproachful voice rang out through the square.

"Ira…," Master Aced whispered.

We weren't out of the woods yet, I knew, but I heaved a sigh of relief anyway.

"Are you not a Master? How could you harm one of our own?!"

"Hmph! I was only testing his strength."

"You intended to do far worse than that. That's why I came here."

Ira and Aced glared at each other angrily. The Foreteller in the bear mask eventually dismissed his Keyblade, and I ran over to you. It was over; Master Aced's fury had turned on Ira now.

"The final battle is inevitable now. Invi, Gula, Ava, and you, too, Ira—your Unions were so desperate to collect more Lux than the others. This war has been going on since the beginning, and you four only made it worse."

Ira remained calm, despite Aced's vehement accusations. "And you intend to end the conflict by force?"

Aced brushed off the question and continued. "The fate of the world is decided by a strong leader. It isn't Lux my Union needs—we need fighters. A strong organization is essential, and only one leader is necessary to protect the balance. I'll banish the four of you and guide all the Unions as one."

Was there no way to get Master Aced to rethink this decision? The cold, harsh reality was setting in: We had passed the point of no return.

"Don't overestimate yourself, Aced," Master Ira retorted. "You don't have the strength for that. I'll show you what comes of such arrogance."

Master Aced turned his back and walked away. "I'll be waiting on the battlefield!" he barked.

Was it already too late? Was this rift irreparable? Would we never stand side by side again?

After that tense exchange, the other Keyblade wielders dispersed. The only ones left were you, me, Skuld, and Master Ira.

"Master Ira?" Skuld asked tremulously. "He mentioned a battlefield… What's going to happen?"

"The fated hour is almost upon us," he replied.

"So it's as Master Ava said…"

"It is inevitable."

"But Master Ava told me there would be no victors in this war. Why fight it at all?!"

"Because…we must ensure there will be no victors." Master Ira seemed almost mournful.

A battle that no one was meant to win? Then what was the point?

You were still on your knees, listening closely to the conversation.

"Prepare yourselves," Master Ira said to us, and then he left in the opposite direction of Master Aced. Once both the Foretellers were gone and the danger had passed, you finally collapsed.

You were dreaming again. Where were you this time? You spied people in the distance. There were one, two, three…nine people in total, standing across from thirteen others clad in coats of purest black. You didn't know who they were or what they wanted.

There was a sudden flash, a great light burning pure and true…

You were still asleep. I watched you with worry, as did Skuld beside me.

"Will he be okay?" I blurted out.

"I'm sure he will. I bet he's just exhausted."

"Thanks for all your help, Skuld."

She had helped bring you home.

She smiled and shook her head. "You know, it's getting worse by the day. I see little standoffs everywhere."

"Yeah…"

"What's going on with the Masters? Well, I suppose we just saw…"

I hung my head. So much was happening that I didn't know. "Yeah… Everyone's in it for themselves now. I don't know what happened, but they've completely changed."

"It's true… There's no way to avoid this war now, is there?" Skuld sighed in defeat.

That was when you suddenly spoke. "Where's Ephemer?"

"Oh!" I looked at you in surprise. How long had you been conscious? "Great! You're awake."

You nodded, still lying in bed. That was one less worry on my mind.

You turned to Skuld and asked your question again. "Did you find Ephemer yet?"

Skuld's eyes wandered for a moment, then chose each word with care as she replied. "Not yet, but I know he's busy with a task from Master Ava. I've been trying to persuade as many Keyblade wielders as I can to stay away from the final battle, but most of them refuse to believe it's even coming... In fact, even the Dandelions are starting to get nervous without Master Ava around, and morale has started to drop..."

"Wait, what happened to Master Ava?" you asked before she could finish. You sounded anxious.

Skuld shook her head, so I decided to tell you what I knew instead.

"The truth is...no one's seen Master Ava for a while now... Master Gula might know something, though. They were friends, after all."

You sat up impatiently, and I knew how you felt. "Let's go ask Master Gula then," you said.

The fated hour is almost upon us, Master Ira had said, but...

"You need to rest more!" I tried my hardest to stop you; you weren't fully healed yet.

Still, you climbed from the bed. "There's no time."

After thinking for a moment, Skuld nodded in agreement. "...You're right."

"But..." I was concerned, though. I was worried for you. After all, you were my friend.

"I'll be all right, Chirithy." You patted me on the head.

"Okay..."

I nodded, still worried, and we left to find Gula.

Daybreak Town by night was infested with Heartless, noticeably more than usual. You could try to thin them out and collect all the Lux you wanted, but there were always more.

"Are we in the right place?" Skuld asked.

"Master Gula doesn't come to the tower often. He tends to spend his time in one of the empty houses around town," I replied.

If you wanted to find him, your best bet was around here, below the bridge in front of the tower.

"I'm pretty sure this is it, but I don't know if he'll be here."

"Let's check anyway."

We entered the vacant house. It was dark inside, and apparently empty.

"It's awfully quiet," I commented as I peered around.

Then someone answered. "Looking for me?"

At pretty much the same moment, Gula in his leopard mask stepped out of the darkness.

"Master Gula!" I yelped in surprise, maybe a little too loudly. I wasn't expecting it to be this easy.

"If you're skipping out on collecting Lux to come here, then you must be part of Ava's Dandelions."

"Um, yes," Skuld replied awkwardly.

"Are you looking for her?" Gula asked, but it was clear he already knew the answer. The Foretellers were so mysterious, so unknowable. It gave me chills.

Skuld's reply was clear and honest. "We are."

"And what will you do if you find her? Will you ask her to change fate and avoid the war? Not even Ava can do that. Or do you just want answers? Because knowledge won't help you here." He raised each point and immediately shot it down, warning us not to pursue a lost cause.

Even so, Skuld still looked him in the eye. "I can't just sit around and wait for the end of the world. I'll save as many of my friends as I can. That's my job as a Dandelion."

"I can certainly see why she would have chosen you. You're just like her—always doing the right thing," Gula remarked half to himself, his gaze lowering briefly. Maybe that last part was meant for Ava herself? "But doing what's right isn't enough to save the world. I don't know if anything is. The only one who could do it would be the Master."

"The Master?" Skuld asked.

"You've heard about him from Chirithy, haven't you? The five Fore-tellers were the apprentices of the Master of Masters. He's the only one who could change our fate now. No one else stands a chance."

The mysterious Master who created me might just be the most powerful person in this world. Gula was right; if anyone could do something about all this, it was him.

"Where is he?" Skuld asked imploringly.

"And there's the rub. The Master just disappeared one day. Ava and I have both tried to find him, but we don't even have a clue to go on. The only one who might know where he went is Luxu."

Master Luxu—I'd heard that name before.

"You know him?" Skuld asked, so I told her what I knew.

"The sixth apprentice. Luxu vanished not long after the Master himself."

Skuld turned back to Master Gula. "And you can't find Master Luxu either?"

The only way out of this was finding a way to contact the Master of Masters. Skuld was trying to follow that tiny thread of hope—but Gula just snickered.

"Of course you would ask that. You really are like Ava." He was still laughing, but we were desperate.

"You mean, Master Ava is…"

Skuld finally put two and two together. The missing Master Ava was already on the hunt…

"Yep. She's already searching for Luxu so she can ask him where to find the Master," Gula answered with a hint of melancholy. He then recited a passage from a book: "Imbalance observed, strength mis-placed, a future filled with sorrow… Words of truth misunderstood as they explore the secret of tomorrow…"

What was that supposed to mean? I had no idea, and Skuld asked him directly. "What's that?"

"A line from the Lost Page… Who could it be referring to…?"

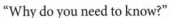

"Why do you need to know?"

"Because this traitor put us on the course to the end of the world."

Skuld gasped.

…"Imbalance observed"—that had to be someone who didn't like having others acting without organization.

…"Strength misplaced, a future filled with sorrow"— Did this line suggest that the traitor cared for others, that there was a certain weakness to them?

Master Gula shrugged his shoulders.

"I thought I knew who it was, but it didn't make a difference. In fact, I've started wondering if I was wrong the whole time."

"'Words of truth misunderstood as they explore the secret of tomorrow…' What do you think that means?"

What was this "truth," and how would it be misunderstood? I didn't know the answer, but the stakes were high. That misunderstanding had brought us to the end of the world.

"There's more." Master Gula began to step away from us.

"'With a single strike, toll the bells and herald the end, bringing war upon us, as fate did intend…'" he recited, then sat down on a crate in a corner of the room.

All of us were silent. I didn't know what to do, but there was one thing that didn't sit right with me.

"Should you really be sharing such an important passage from the Book of Prophecies with us?"

"Not really, but the future's already set in stone, so I doubt it matters anymore," the Foreteller said. In his mind, it was already too late.

Just then, the bell tolled. Was this the signal for the final battle…?

"See? It's beginning." Gula laughed softly, though it was hard to tell whether he was saddened or amused.

"The fated hour…?" Skuld asked. Were we… Were we too late?

"You should head back. Your Union might be calling you soon," Master Gula said, and then disappeared.

*   *   *

Right around then, on the outskirts of Daybreak Town, Ava stood atop a hill that almost no one ever visited. In front of her was a man in a black coat sitting on the grass, legs splayed, and observing the city.

"I finally found you, Luxu."

"Well, if it isn't Ava...," replied the man called Luxu, not turning to face her.

"What have you been doing all this time?" the Foreteller asked suspiciously, stepping closer.

"Watching," he replied simply.

That made no sense to her. "What?"

"That's my role," Luxu replied, his eyes still on the town. He had apparently come to terms with this some time ago.

"What was your role?" Ava asked. She couldn't begin to guess how the Master's orders would have led him to this.

But Luxu's answer was far from helpful. "To watch."

"Huh?"

"Just to watch."

...In fact, it was the same.

"What do you mean?"

He was shamelessly refusing to give a straight answer, and Ava wasn't having it. But when she pushed further, he slowly got to his feet.

"Unlike you five, I didn't get a copy of a Book of Prophecies. Instead, I have to move forward into the future the Book describes. I'll watch this world end, then set off into the next one."

"Huh...?" Ava was speechless. What was the Master of Masters really after?

She was clearly confused, so Luxu decided to enlighten her. "You want to avoid the Keyblade War, right? And since I up and vanished just like the Master, you thought if you came looking for me, you

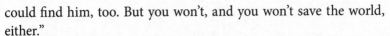

could find him, too. But you won't, and you won't save the world, either."

Stunned, Ava could feel despair stealing across her heart, but still she forced herself to speak. "Luxu, what do you know?"

The man in the black coat slowly ambled over toward her. "The Lost Page... What's written there is a prophecy that none of you know. The Master's true intentions."

Luxu was giving her the pieces, but Ava struggled to assemble them.

Because that would mean...

"True intentions? Are you saying the Master meant for things to turn out this way? That he wanted the world to end?"

"My role is to carry on the secret. The Lost Page laid out a path for this world, and I have to keep it on course. As for the Master's true intentions, he doesn't really care how this world ends up. He's just watching and making sure I can fulfill my mission."

Ava tensed up slightly as Luxu drew closer. "What's written on the Lost Page?" she asked.

Luxu's lips curled up into a little smile at that question.

"Luxu... Are you the one behind all this? Are you the traitor?"

Instead of answering her accusation, he summoned his Keyblade.

A Keyblade that would be used by another in a world far, far away...

Luxu whispered something into Ava's ear.

"But..." Ava trembled at the answer he gave.

"There, you see? That's your traitor. Can you accept the truth?"

She could sense Luxu giving her a hard look from within his hood.

"That's why you need to accept your fate and join the battle. Even if there is another answer, it's on the other side of this fight. Don't you think the Master is less invested in the future of the world and more in learning where his apprentices' hearts will guide them?"

Ava's expression contorted with pain and shock.

"He's more invested in us than in the world? That can't be! Luxu... you're twisting the Master's will. He would never wish for this!"

Ava called her own Keyblade to her hand.

*   *   *

And the bell tolled.

The Master of Masters bequeathed the Keyblade to Luxu.

Luxu gazed at the weapon intently, while the Master returned to his seat, propped his elbow on the desk, and observed his apprentice. The two of them wore the same black coats, but the Master was taller—so much taller that sitting down only brought him to Luxu's eye level.

"The Gazing Eye?" asked Luxu.

The weapon had something that resembled an eyeball embedded in the blade. Maybe it was some kind of gem carved to look that way, Luxu thought.

"That's not what it's called," the Master replied with a touch of humor in his voice.

"Oh, what then?" Luxu looked relieved for some reason.

"Hmm. Actually, there's no name," the Master of Masters quipped lightly.

"No Name..." Luxu stared intently at the Keyblade.

"Well, 'gazing' or not, that Keyblade does have an eye in it. My eye, to be exact."

Luxu cringed away. "Ew!" he yelped.

"Oh, you think that's gross, do ya?" the Master of Masters asked, offended.

"N-no!" Luxu furiously denied the claim; he respected his teacher too much for that.

"Yeah, sure. Anyway, about your role. You need to pass down that Keyblade to your apprentice, and then him to his, so that my eye can see the future."

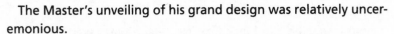

The Master's unveiling of his grand design was relatively unceremonious.

...But Luxu understood. "So the Book of Prophecies...," he murmured.

The Master raised his pointer finger. "Bingo!" He then pointed that finger at Luxu.

"The fact that it exists is proof of your success! That means you've trained a worthy apprentice, passed down that handsome Keyblade, and fulfilled your role! Congratulations!"

While the Master of Masters clapped his hands to celebrate Luxu's past achievements in the future, Luxu himself merely stared in surprise at the Keyblade.

"What's the matter? Come on, you did a fantastic job! At least smile a little!"

Luxu only grew more confused. "But I haven't done anything yet...," he said. To him, there was no reason for celebration, and certainly no sense of accomplishment.

"Good point. Guess you better get started then! Unfortunately, you'll have to go alone from here on out. No Book of Prophecies to keep you company, either. I can't have you causing any temporal paradoxes. But, hey, we both know you'll do just fine without it, right?"

However, there were other apprentices besides Luxu who were also in training.

"Do I really have to go alone? What about the others?" he asked.

The Master of Masters laughed off the idea. "Minor details, so don't sweat it. For now, you, that Keyblade, and...this box need to stay out of sight."

The Master of Masters pulled out a black box so large that lugging it around would prove challenging. The edges were decorated with a silver pattern, and it also had handles.

"Just watch with your own eyes—and my eye, of course—as things unfold between the others. Then when the time is right, go off and do your thing."

"What's in it?"

Luxu inspected the black box. No telling what was inside this box of mysteries. The Master had to have entrusted it to him for some special purpose.

"It's a secret. And, well, you see...the thing is...you can never, ever open it."

"Great, now I really wanna know," Luxu said back. The Master seemed as lighthearted as ever, but he often joked around when he was talking about matters of grave importance. This time was no different.

"Ah, all right. I'll indulge you. But this secret stays between the two of us, and you have to promise never to open the box."

"I promise."

The Master leaned in toward Luxu, then whispered to his apprentice through his hood. Luxu gasped, then looked up at his teacher. "But, why?"

The Master met the question with a meaningful smile. "You'll see."

He was back to his old tricks again.

But still, why that, of all things?

Luxu regarded the Master of Masters, unable to conceal his bewilderment.

Chapter 9

WE RETURNED TO THE TOP OF THE BRIDGE FROM
Gula's hideout, unsure of what we should even say to each other now.

The whole town was abuzz, but not in the usual way.

"Anyway, I'm going back to the other Dandelions," said Skuld. "Come with?"

Your gaze sank to the ground, and you shook your head no.

"It's okay. I understand. Just…don't fight when the time comes, okay? I want you to journey to the world outside with us, and I'm sure Ephemer would, too. Think it over."

You nodded weakly. The inevitable, fated battle was coming, but not even I knew what choice you would make when it arrived.

"Well…see you later." Skuld held out her hand to you with loneliness in her eyes. You clasped it in your own, only you were smiling. She couldn't help but smile back.

Eventually, you let go, and she hurried on her way.

I looked anxiously up at you. "Are you all right?"

You nodded.

My only choice was to have faith in the path you had chosen. "Okay, then… Let's head home," I said with a nod of my own, and then we climbed the steps toward our house. We wouldn't survive the battle to come if we didn't rest at least a little—if fighting through it was even the right thing to do.

"Chirithy…," you said.

"Huh?" I looked back at you.

"If I vanish, what happens to you?" You almost never spoke; this question was especially important. The answer would mean a lot to you.

My head drooped.

"Will you disappear?"

"Yeah…"

"Oh…"

The thought of that made me sad, but the idea of it happening to *you* was so much worse. You honestly were…

"What do you think, Chirithy? What should I do?" I could hear the pain in your voice. Your eyes were downcast.

"I don't want you to disappear," I replied. "It may not be what the Foretellers intended, but I'm your friend, not just your familiar, and I don't want you to fight." That was how I truly felt.

We were friends, after all. I ran over to you, and you picked me up and gave me a big hug.

"Thanks…," you said, even though I was the one who was grateful. But then…

"Whaaat? You're not gonna fight?"

A voice came from up at the top of the steps. We separated and looked up to see the dark Chirithy.

"You gonna run away with the Dandelions?"

"You again. And the Dandelions aren't running," I retorted.

However, he responded by saying, "Yeah, yeah, something about keeping the Keybearers around into the future?" he replied. "You've probably already realized this, but doesn't that mean abandoning a lot of your friends?"

"Who are you?" you asked. The black Chirithy snickered.

"You've been gathering the sins of this world into that bangle for a long time now, and you're finally starting to convert it into dark power."

"Sins?" you replied.

"Yep. You all called it 'Guilt,' but darkness by any other name is just as sweet."

"That can't be…," I said quietly. I'd never heard of Guilt being the power of darkness.

"It's all right," the dark Chirithy continued mockingly. "You must know that this is just another part of our Master's plan?"

"You're wrong—that bangle is supposed to convert those sins to light…," I pleaded desperately, repeating the same explanation that had been given to me.

The corrupted Chirithy just cackled. "Well then, how do you explain me? Why was I born? Did the Master fail to predict me, too?" He sneered.

We hung our heads. *It can't be… That shouldn't be possible.*

"Come on, haven't you figured out what I am by now? I was born from *your* darkness. I'm *your* Chirithy, kid."

After his announcement, the black Chirithy teleported from the street to a rooftop. We looked up at him in disbelief.

"That's a lie!" I shouted. You only had one guide—me.

"At this point, what difference does it make if I'm lying or not? You see, I'm different from that Chirithy—I'm not always by your side, and I can do what I want."

Just then, three monsters with black wings and clothing of the same color appeared. You had faced them before. They were Keyblade wielders that had succumbed to darkness.

They moved to surround us.

"What in the world?!"

"If you won't join the final battle, then I'm going to show you *my* dream," declared the dark Chirithy.

You immediately called upon your Keyblade.

"If you're really his Chirithy, then why?!" Despite the danger, I had to ask.

If you disappeared, then so would I—and if the dark Chirithy really did belong to you, then so would he.

The dark Chirithy was still grinning, though. "Unlike you Spirits, we Nightmares exist to show bad dreams. We break all those connections tying us down so we can live free."

"Spirit? Nightmare...?"

I remembered hearing about Nightmares from the Master, but this new information from the dark Chirithy puzzled me. *Nightmares are free...?*

Behind me, your battle had already begun.

You struggled to block and repel the attacks of the dark creatures that circled around you.

Were these the same ones that you had fought together with Skuld, or were they another set of Keyblade wielders that had fallen under the sway of darkness? They seemed much more dangerous than before—but then again, so were you.

You cast a spell with your Keyblade, which became a burst of light that sent the monsters flying. They didn't get up again.

"You've gotten strong, huh? I'm glad," commented the dark Chirithy as he moved from the roof back to the street. As the bodies of the fallen creatures and the dark Chirithy both rose into the air, a dark miasma rippled across them. "Now, let's really see what you're made of."

As the creatures floated toward the black Chirithy, the dark aura consumed them, and the corrupted Dream Eater gradually swelled into something so enormous it didn't resemble a Chirithy at all anymore. It was just a monster, a great and terrible horror with large black wings, huge arms with vicious claws, and wolflike jaws filled with sharp fangs.

We gasped.

From the dark cloud, a black light lanced out at you at blinding speed. You deflected one of the beams, then charged straight at the Nightmare and wounded its wings. Still, it managed to flap into the air to get momentum for a diving attack.

The beast's strength was overwhelming; this was a whole different level from the three fallen Keyblade wielders you fought a moment ago. It might have been even stronger than the Foretellers.

Was this the power of darkness—the power of darkness *you* had collected?

I was a Spirit, and the dark Chirithy was a Nightmare. Where and how had our paths diverged? I didn't know. Why had you created darkness? Who was behind this? What did they want?

You hit the dark Chirithy with everything you could muster.

Who knew whether that strength came from Guilt or from light? I certainly didn't. All I knew was that I didn't want you to disappear—not for my own sake, but for yours. I wanted you to live.

The dark Chirithy finally went still, then transformed back into his original form. He fell to the ground, where a black smoke rose from his body.

"Now, our bond is broken," he said.

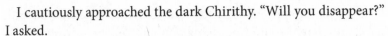

I cautiously approached the dark Chirithy. "Will you disappear?" I asked.

"For now. Let's meet in another dream…"

And with those parting words, the corrupted Chirithy slowly faded from existence along with the darkness around him.

Another dream? What did he mean by that?

…A few days after that, we arrived in the wasteland that would later come to be known as the Keyblade Graveyard.

Even in the most hopeless of circumstances, people still want to hold on to a ray of hope, to those last threads of their dream, up until the very end. I had to believe that was why you had chosen to be here.

Each of the Foretellers and the members of their respective Unions had all assembled to discuss something.

This was beyond our power to solve. The battle—the final battle predicted in the Book of Prophecies—was beginning.

We didn't listen to a word the Foretellers said. Maybe they were discussing what was about to happen here—what was going to unfold before our eyes.

Everyone held their Keyblades aloft and raised their voices in a battle cry. Then, they charged.

What was about to begin here? What was about to end?

The air was strangely electric; every sight, every sound is indelibly etched in my memory.

There was no time to think about the why of this battle. The foes before you were not the little monsters you were used to facing. They were former comrades.

Countless hearts rose from the fallen Keyblade wielders and floated into the sky.

Rain began to fall.

You directed your gaze skyward, and tears slid down your cheeks alongside the raindrops.

"This isn't the end," you whispered.

Master Aced appeared, his Keyblade drawn, and fixed you with a baleful glare. "You!" Not giving you any chance to respond, he launched himself toward you and brought his blade down. The terrifying wind generated by the blow whipped past your cheek.

"Didn't I tell you before? You are unworthy, boy."

It was a cruel thing to say, but you answered by readying your Keyblade.

"And still you wish to do battle? Such strength of will would be a great asset to my Union."

Aced punctuated his confident remark by knocking you away with a single strike.

But you weren't ready to give up just yet. You scrambled to your feet and sprang into the air, raising your Keyblade with arms that were twigs compared to Master Aced's, and barely grazed his torso. The bear-masked Foreteller leaped back, and you closed the gap, slashing at him while he checked each and every blow. Eventually, the two of you broke apart.

"Incredible! You are worthy after all! You are strong! Wonderfully strong!" he cried with pleasure.

I'd never seen Aced with such a smile. Nothing made sense anymore.

"Which is why you must disappear, here and now, before you can become a threat!"

Master Aced brought down his Keyblade in a blow more powerful than any before it, and it took everything you had to dodge. He came after you over and over, but each time, you managed to avoid his strikes.

You couldn't find an opening to launch a counterattack—or so you thought, when suddenly, Aced's Keyblade was stopped by another's.

It was Master Ira.

"Iraaa!!"

"Let us settle this, once and for all."

Aced's eyes burned with fury as he looked at the one who had protected you. Master Ira glanced at you for the briefest of moments, then leaped into the air. Aced followed him, and the two Foretellers vanished into the wasteland.

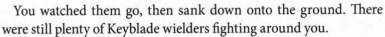

You watched them go, then sank down onto the ground. There were still plenty of Keyblade wielders fighting around you.

"It's not over yet...," you whispered to yourself. That was when you spotted someone—Master Gula. You sprang to your feet and burst into a run.

"Hey, I remember you...," the Foreteller said, pointing at you. He seemed as carefree as ever, even as other Keybearers fought for their lives around him. "You look a little worse for wear. You okay?"

He was right; you were exhausted, but you nodded that you were fine.

"So we can get down to business?" Master Gula swung his Keyblade at you lightly, and you answered with your own. "That's the spirit. This is a war, after all."

A smile appeared on his lips, and then he closed the distance between you in the blink of an eye. His movements were so smooth and quick, you could barely keep up. Still, you successfully blocked his Keyblade and turned the tables with an attack of your own. You did your best to keep after Gula as he darted gracefully about the barren landscape, but when you tried magic instead, he only deflected the spell.

"Whoa, you're tough! I didn't come here to run myself ragged fighting you. No thanks," Master Gula said, dismissing his Keyblade. "See you around."

He then disappeared to somewhere with all of the same speed and agility from before.

You plopped down on the spot again. Nothing around had changed since your last fight; Keyblade wielders were fighting, wounding each other, and falling. And when they fell, their hearts floated up from their bodies and faded away.

You reached out for one of these hearts, but it slid through your trembling grasp, and drifted up into the sky.

"No! You can't go...," you cried out mournfully to the rainy heavens. So many hearts were vanishing into those dark clouds.

"You..."

The voice belonged to Master Ira. Maybe he had lost track of Master Aced, or maybe their duel was already over? Now, he was watching the sky like you. I wondered what was going through his mind right then.

"I will ensure you go peacefully…," he said, but his hand remained at his side.

You jumped to your feet and tightened your grip on your weapon. You charged, but Master Ira simply stepped out of the way with ease. Still, you kept after him, giving it all you had.

Finally, your Keyblade landed a solid hit—or so you thought, when you realized he had finally summoned his weapon. A second later, he knocked you away. You came crashing to the ground, but you were on your feet again in no time.

"You've grown much. Well done. It's a shame to lose a wielder like you. Truly a shame."

Master Ira took slow, measured steps toward you and struck down with his Keyblade.

This time, I thought you were really, truly done for, but then someone attacked Master Ira from behind—it was Master Aced.

Master Ira spun around and stopped the Keyblade.

"I've long awaited this moment, Ira…"

Sparks flew as their Keyblades clashed together again and again.

"Aced…!" For the first time, Master Ira showed signs of anger as he checked an especially powerful strike.

"I'll rebuild this world as its new leader!" his opponent roared, and something inside Master Ira seemed to snap.

"Had you not upset the balance, there would be no need!" He slashed out at Master Aced, and their vicious duel carried them to another part of the battlefield.

You slowly fell to the ground again—how many times was this now? You were near the end of your rope, I'm sure. Masterless Keyblades had been driven into the earth all around you, while a multitude of hearts drifted up into the sky.

The downpour became a torrent that soaked you to the bone,

and I could hear the pain in your ragged breaths. You jammed your Keyblade into the ground, using it as support to help you stand upright.

Slowly, you began stumbling forward, because there was someone ahead of you.

"You're..."

Master Ava.

"I looked everywhere for you," you said, but the Foreteller avoided your gaze. "Why are you here, Master Ava? Did you come to stop the war, or...?"

Her eyes remained lowered, but her Keyblade thrust out toward you. You swallowed hard.

"...Raise your weapon."

"What happened...?" you asked, but Master Ava only raised her head and shouted.

"Raise your blade and fight!"

She brought down her Keyblade in the same instant, casting a spell that hit its mark. You did your best to weather the impact, but each attack was taking its toll. You still held your head high, rushed at Master Ava, and swung your Keyblade at her. She parried the blow, and the impact pushed you away from each other.

Your shoulders heaved with each breath; you were struggling now. Still, you weren't about to give up. You charged at Master Ava once more, and when she blocked the strike, you were rebuffed yet again for I don't know how many times.

"Why?" you gasped through labored breaths, ready to collapse at any moment.

"Some secrets aren't for you to know... Leave this place. Go with the Dandelions," Master Ava said as she dismissed her Keyblade and walked away.

At this point, all you could do was watch her leave, but not for long. Your eyelids fell closed, and you collapsed.

I ran over to you and clung to your chest. "It's all right. You've done enough."

You opened your eyes slowly, your breath faint, and patted my head.

Then the rain stopped. A ray of light pierced through a break in the clouds.

Countless scores of Keyblades were stuck into the wasteland, but none of their wielders were anywhere to be found.

...And time passed.

An approaching silhouette appeared in the distance.

"Is it my time...?" you whispered. To your fading consciousness, she must have seemed like a vision of the afterlife.

Or maybe you weren't seeing anything at all by that point? I was starting to grow worried, when—

"Skuld...," you murmured her name, smiling faintly.

She said your name as well.

When you saw who was standing next to her, tears welled in your eyes and spilled over. "We made...a promise..."

It was Ephemer. "I didn't forget," he said warmly. You smiled, too.

At last, you were reunited.

"You're late...," you whispered.

"I know. I'm sorry..." Ephemer held out his hand to you, and you held out yours. "We'll go together." He tried to help you up from the ground.

Light filled the world until it was impossible to recognize anything. Anything at all.

You don't remember any of it now. The only thing you saw was a slightly unnerving dream.

You're just going to take a little nap.

What kind of world will greet you when you wake? Will it be everything you hoped for?

The answer to that is up to you.

EPILOGUE–UNCHAINED χ

RAIN WAS FALLING OVER THE WASTELAND.

Here, many Keyblade wielders had done battle, divided into friend and foe.

I'd learned their faces, some of them; with others, I'd even exchanged words. They had all worked their hardest to complete their mission.

How had this happened? Why had it come to this?

I walked the wasteland alone.

Some time ago, back when I never would have believed such a tragedy could come to pass, the Master of Masters bestowed another role upon me, in addition to forming the Dandelions.

"Union leaders?"

This task had been assigned to five people in this world, including myself.

"When all's said and done, and only the Dandelions are left, they'll need to lead the Unions."

Five people, the same number as us. But—

"Is there a need to maintain the Unions?" The Dandelions were formed from Keybearers who shared a common goal, regardless of their original Unions; I couldn't imagine why we'd want to divide them again. It would pull the members of differing Unions away from each other, potentially even leading to conflict. Wouldn't we want to avoid this in the new world?

"Of course! Getting rid of them would be like pooh-poohing all your hard work!"

And yet, the Master seemed to believe they were necessary even in the world to come, and I was in no position to contradict him.

"Besides, other than the five new Union leaders, no one else is going to know that the world...well, you know."

"What?"

I had yet to accept the idea that the world was going to end at all, but the Master spoke as if it was a given. *Are the prophecies so absolute?* I wondered. *Is there no changing fate?*

"There's no point for anyone to carry around knowledge of such a catastrophic event. I want everyone to start over in a different world with a clean slate—well, to their knowledge, of course."

"You can do that?"

A "catastrophic event"—the war that existed only in prophecies, but was destined to arrive very soon.

"Apparently so. Here, take a look at these five names." The Master handed me a paper with the names of five Keyblade wielders. I knew a few of them. "They're your new recruits. Make them all Dandelions, and when the time comes, teach them their roles."

One of the names was specially marked.

"Why is this one circled in red?"

"Jackpot! That lucky wielder gets their own free copy of the Book of Prophecies!"

"The Book?"

"Yeah, it's a great read, don't you think? Oh, and it's also needed to shape the world into what it's supposed to be."

The Book of Prophecies didn't simply predict the future—it also allowed future worlds to manifest in this one.

"That sounds awfully risky," I commented.

"Only if the other four get their hands on it. Ava, this book needs to be handed to its owner in secret. No one else can know."

"All right."

I had no choice but to nod and accept the tome, full of events yet to come.

As I returned from my reverie, I saw that boy right in front of me—Ephemer's friend from Anguis.

"You're…"

He was exceptional; I had crossed Keyblades with him, spoken with him several times, and even asked him to join the Dandelions. Yet he had chosen to remain in the battlefield.

He had plunged his Keyblade into the ground to steady himself.

"I looked everywhere for you. Why are you here, Master Ava? Did you come to stop the war, or…?"

He was wandering around out here in search of me?! Unfortunately, I had no answers for his questions.

"…Raise your weapon," I said.

"What happened…?" he asked, and I couldn't stop myself from shouting back.

"Raise your blade and fight!"

I remember talking to Ephemer, one of the Keyblade wielders selected to become a Union leader in the Dandelions.

We were on top of a hill outside of Daybreak Town with an excellent view of our home.

I told Ephemer what the Master had told me. "This secret must stay with the five of you. When all is said and done, you must come to the fated land. You'll be joined by four others."

I had already spoken to the others; Ephemer was the last.

My heart was still slightly unsteady as I explained. Was there truly no way to avoid this?

But no matter how I felt about it, I had to tell him. "We cannot avoid the end." He raised his head, and I continued. "Not even the Masters, including myself, are likely to survive."

"Me? A Master? A Union leader?" he protested, stunned. "That's crazy. And what's this nonsense about 'the end'?" I would never dream of arguing with my own Master this way; that honesty was something I loved about Ephemer.

"There isn't much time left. You are the ones who will remain.

Someone needs to keep everything and everyone in order. Otherwise, light will expire," I informed him, just I had been instructed.

"But..."

Of course, he was hesitant to accept this; anyone would be. It was too sudden. I had been the same.

"There will be four others from the Dandelions. The five of you will each lead a Union, as the five of us have. You won't be alone in this. The five of you can work together."

"The five of us..."

I handed Ephemer a notebook. "There are rules the five of you must obey when you become leaders of your own Unions."

He accepted the book quizzically. "I'm listening, but this whole conversation about the end and leading Unions and all... I'm still trying to wrap my head around it."

"As long as you keep listening."

That was all I could say for now, mainly because I didn't want to accept this turn of events, either.

"...Okay." Ephemer nodded stiffly.

"What I need you to do is to prepare for the other world. I'll be sending all the Dandelions there soon. You'll continue living your lives, but without the impending doom."

This other world was a copy of this world as it was written in the Book of Prophecies, with only two differences: no Foretellers, and no future apocalypse. In place of Foretellers, it would have five new Union leaders.

"So it's like an alternate reality?"

"Yes. But in order for it to work, the Dandelions will need to forget the strife, the war."

Ephemer looked slightly taken aback. "So they won't remember any of it?" He lowered his head, mulling over the implications. He didn't quite get it.

"There's no need for them to remember such a tragedy. It'll simply be a burden. Only the five of you will know the truth. The Chirithy of each wielder will make it happen."

"It might be a burden, but isn't it better they remember the past? The past is what makes the future," Ephemer said, looking up.

That was true. Normally that might be the best course of action. But...

"I thought you might say that. But I wonder if you would feel the same if you were there to witness the end."

Back then, I still hoped that end would never arrive.

But it did, and here we were.

I remember wondering to myself: *If everyone is fighting during the world's final moments...what will I be doing?*

I slashed my Keyblade downward, casting a spell that struck home.

The boy did his best to weather the impact. He was already on his last legs, and yet he kept his head high and came at me again. He swung his Keyblade at me, and I blocked the blow. The impact knocked us both backward.

He wasn't giving up. He rushed at me yet again; I blocked and drove him back. Over and over, the cycle repeated.

"Why?" he gasped through labored breaths, ready to collapse at any moment.

"Some secrets aren't meant to be known... Get away from here. Go with the Dandelions," I answered. This boy was not meant to vanish. He had a heart of light that could prevail over darkness. I put away my Keyblade.

But then...where was I supposed to go?

Let the wind carry you far, far away...my Dandelions.

The war was over, a blue sky unfurled above.

The barren terrain was pierced by too many Keyblades to count. Each one was another wielder lost.

Ephemer stopped and looked up at the sky. It had been pouring on the day of the battle, but now the sky was clear. You'd think the weather right after an apocalypse would be dark and oppressive, but maybe it wasn't. Maybe it was just this: gentle breezes and clear skies stretching off into eternity.

And the world hadn't been destroyed.

Ephemer stood in a crossroads formed by the paths between fields of Keyblades—the place they had promised to meet.

"Am I the second to arrive?"

Ephemer knew that voice. He turned to face the one who had spoken. "Skuld? Well, this is a surprise!"

"Disappointed? I, on the other hand, had a feeling you might be here," she replied with a grin.

"Of course not! We came here once right after the war, remember? I just never thought I'd see you here again," he replied, and Skuld shrugged.

"This whole thing is a big secret. We weren't supposed to tell anybody."

"I suppose you're right." Ephemer nodded in response.

So Skuld had been able to keep the secret, just like Master Ava asked.

"I wonder who the others are," she commented.

"I dunno," Ephemer replied. "I wasn't sure I believed Master Ava when she said others would come. But now that you're here..." Just then, another figure arrived at the edge of the wastes.

"Look! Someone's coming," Skuld exclaimed before running to meet the newcomer. "Welcome! You're number three. I'm Skuld. Nice to meet you."

"Oh, uh, thanks. You too."

The one who answered was a boy with short, wavy golden hair and a tendency to look at the ground. He seemed so quiet that it was hard to imagine him fighting with a Keyblade.

Ephemer walked up to him. "So, Master Ava talked to you too, huh?"

"Yeah, she said I should come here when everything was over, and that I was one of the five."

"I got the same speech. I'm Ephemer, by the way." Ephemer extended a hand, and the boy responded in kind and gave it a firm shake.

"I'm Ventus. Call me Ven," he said shyly. "You two know each other, huh?"

"We've seen each other around before, I guess," Skuld replied and smiled at Ephemer.

"Must be nice; I've always been on my own."

"I was pretty much on my own, too." Skuld came closer. The time she spent with Ephemer hadn't actually been that long at all.

"I wonder why I was chosen for this," Ven said, uncertain of himself. "I'm not especially good at anything… And I'm never at the top of the rankings."

He's got a point… Why were any of us chosen?

Ephemer thought it over. Unlike other Keyblade wielders, he had always asked questions and tried to find the answers to them. Maybe that was why, and if so, perhaps Skuld was the same way.

So what about the other leaders?

Ephemer had never seen this boy Ven. Many Keyblade wielders he would at least recognize by face, and you usually heard stories about the really exceptional ones, but Ven belonged to neither category.

"I'm sure Master Ava has her reasons," Skuld said, offering the only answer she had.

"You think so?" asked Ven. "I don't know her all that much. I've barely spoken with her."

"She's easy to talk to, that's for sure," Ephemer said wistfully. He had no idea what she was up to now. Had everyone else truly been lost?

"You say that about everyone," Skuld laughed.

"Not true!" Ephemer shot back.

"I sure wish I had friends," Ven muttered as he watched them banter, and Ephemer and Skuld glanced at each other.

"You do!" Ephemer reassured him. "Right here."

"Yeah!" A smile appeared on Ven's face.

"Friends. Cool," murmured an unfamiliar voice, and the three of them turned to see who it was.

There stood a boy with fairly long black hair in a hat of nearly the same color. His clothes were all black, too, creating a strong impression for a strong personality. The boy flashed a set of white teeth in a pleasant, albeit somewhat mischievous smile.

"You must be number four," Skuld said.

The boy nodded and introduced himself. "The name's Brain. Pleasure." He gave another toothy grin. "Thought I'd be the last to arrive. Guess I'm not so lazy after all," he commented with a hint of surprise.

"I guess not," Ephemer said with a laugh.

Brain abruptly turned to him. "So, you the leader?" he asked.

Startled, Ephemer took a sharp breath, but he ultimately kept his smile in place. "No, we haven't decided any of that yet. I think we should wait until we're all here."

"You got it," Brain replied, although he had more questions. "Hey, about the rules. Think they're set in stone? Or more like a guideline?"

Skuld had the answer to that one. "They're the rules. Of course they're set in stone."

"I get it. You're the serious one. Like Master Ava." He shrugged.

Skuld shrugged back. "You're not the first person to say that," she remarked, but her eyes turned a little distant as she spoke.

"I thought you seemed familiar," Ven chimed in.

The other members were starting to wonder about Ven—he hadn't interacted much with Master Ava, so why had he been chosen...?

But Ephemer chose that moment to start teasing Skuld. "But Master Ava's so amazing!"

"What does that mean?"

Everyone giggled at Skuld's angry response, and their doubts about Ven fell to the wayside. After everyone had a good laugh, Brain slowly spoke up again. "But seriously, how do we know we

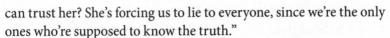

can trust her? She's forcing us to lie to everyone, since we're the only ones who're supposed to know the truth."

"Yeah, I'm not sure how I feel about it either," Ven agreed.

"But...," Ephemer started and then stopped, struggling to find the words.

Skuld looked over to him as he crossed his arms and closed his eyes.

"I thought you might say that. But I wonder if you would feel the same if you were there to witness the end."

Those final moments, when everyone vanished.

"Rules are rules. I don't want anyone else to have to carry the burden of the past," Ephemer opened his eyes and said, making sure to meet the eyes of the other three leaders.

"Got it. I trust you'll guide us down the right path." Brain grinned.

Ven was the next to speak up: "Same here!"

Skuld smiled with relief.

"Just one more," Ephemer declared, then looked out across the barren landscape.

[Playback]

I have a secret. This is my favorite spot that nobody knows about. It belongs to me, Strelitzia.

I was on top of a roof that looked down over the Fountain Square. I always watched the goings-on in the town from here, holding my Chirithy close.

I kept my bangs in place with a few clips, but my two red pigtails were free to blow in the wind. The hem of my dress and the black ribbon at my chest fluttered, too.

These past two years, I fought darkness to protect the light. I made friends, but I also had to say good-bye. I saw new party members come and go. Only a few of my friends from the beginning are still around.

A lot has changed over time, but there has always been one constant in my life—you. I first saw you at Fountain Square. You were waiting for someone, but they never came. When I returned from my mission that day, you were still there—waiting.

You looked so disappointed. I saw your eyes well up as you hugged Chirithy.

Since that day, I began to see you everywhere. It was strange because we must've crossed paths so many times before... But I didn't really notice you until that day.

I wanted to say hi...but I could never muster up the courage.

While everyone was going about their days without question, you began to doubt your mission, your purpose. You saw there was something more, something we weren't being told. You don't know me, but I feel like I know you.

I hope that one day we can be friends. There's so much I'd like to tell you.

It was just another day, and I was walking through town when someone called out to me.

"Strelitzia."

I turned around to see Master Ava.

"I need to ask a favor. It's something only you—a Dandelion—can help me with."

"Me? A-are you sure?"

Master Ava held out a notebook.

That night I was back in my room flipping through the notebook.

"Me, a Union leader...," I murmured.

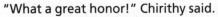

"What a great honor!" Chirithy said.

I still couldn't believe what Master Ava had told me. "Yes. But it's also a great responsibility." My chest was filled with worries.

"I have faith in Master Ava," Chirithy said encouragingly.

"Me too. But what she said about the world... Could that be true?" That was the hardest part of this to believe.

"It's a scary thought, isn't it?"

Chirithy seemed troubled, too. He must have had the same concerns as I did.

I had been asked to join the Dandelions just a short time earlier. The Dandelions were a special Union, different from the other five, which meant—

"Only the Dandelions will survive. That means everyone else will disappear."

I hoped that my prediction wouldn't come true.

"I suppose you're right. But your friends are all Dandelions. Why are you so worried?"

Because I had friends from before I was a Dandelion, too. "They are, but what about everyone else?" I just couldn't accept the idea that so many of us would be lost.

"I know you care. But what do you think would happen if you told everyone the truth? The world is nearing its end, and the Foretellers will disappear. No one would believe you."

"No, they wouldn't..." I didn't even believe it myself—or maybe I just didn't want to. But Master Ava herself had told me about it, so it had to be true.

...What about him?

I jumped to my feet.

"Whoa! Wh-what is it?" Chirithy cried out in surprise.

"He's not a Dandelion!" I exclaimed.

"Wha—? Who?" Chirithy was flustered, but after taking a moment to collect his thoughts, he knew. "Oh, that Keyblade wielder you're always watching."

He realized I meant you—the one always on my mind.

"I have to tell him!" I made for the door of my room, but then I came to a halt. How was I going to find you? It was night, after all.

Okay, I'll just wait until tomorrow. I dashed back into bed.

"What? I thought—"

Chirithy looked at me curiously.

"I'm going to wake up early and wait for him at the Fountain Square," I told him. My mind was made up.

"But Master Ava told you not to say a word to anyone."

"I'm gonna recruit him to the Dandelions. I won't say a word about anything else. Good night!" I said quickly, then closed my eyes.

I have to see you tomorrow!

I was waiting in the Fountain Square when Chirithy came running over from a ways away.

"Good news!" he called. "I saw him over there."

"Thanks!" I dashed off. As I looked around where Chirithy had shown me, I came across a small house along a canal. If you weren't outside, then maybe...

I stepped into the house, but it was empty.

"Maybe my eyes were playing tricks on me," Chirithy said, worried.

"Hello! Is anyone here?" I called out. There was no response.

"Hello?" Chirithy did the same. Nothing. "I guess I was wrong."

I stopped and turned around. "Well, it was worth a shot. I'll head back to the Fountain Square."

"Okay. I'll keep searching." Then Chirithy saw something behind me. "Hmm?"

I noticed his reaction and turned around.

"What?"

*   *   *

That was when I lost consciousness.

When I came to, I couldn't move. I knew I was probably injured, but I didn't feel any pain. I didn't even know where the wound might be—it all happened so fast.

I saw a hand pick up the notebook I received from Master Ava, but even that was getting hazy.

"Strelitzia...," I heard Chirithy say my name.

My body wouldn't quite move how I wanted it to, but I managed to sit up and pull him closer. I was sure he was hurting, too.

"I'm sorry," I whispered, hugging him tight. "This is all my fault..."

"Don't apologize. It's okay," he said in a small voice.

I'm sorry, Chirithy. I know that when I disappear, you will, too. I wish...I'd had the courage.

The final member never seemed to arrive.

"How much longer are they gonna be?" Brain grumbled.

Ven had sat down on the ground beside him, tired of waiting. "Not much longer, I hope."

Ephemer uncrossed his arms and rolled his shoulders. "I'm gonna take a look around," he said, getting ready to walk into the wilderness. In this vast wasteland, it wasn't hard to imagine the fifth leader was nearby and had simply lost their way.

"I'll join you... Oh!" Skuld exclaimed as she was about to go with him. "Someone's coming."

In the distance, a silhouette was slowly approaching. "I hope I didn't keep you waiting," he called.

"Well, you did. How do you plan on making it up to us, Number Five?" Brain replied with a grin as he walked up to meet the new arrival.

Number Five had reddish, relatively long hair that was reminiscent of a flower. His outfit was simple—a white shirt with a black vest—that just made his hair all the more eye-catching. He carried himself gracefully, and looked to be a tad older than Skuld and the rest.

"Number Five? Then I must be the last one," the newcomer said, although his late arrival didn't seem to bother her.

Ephemer stepped forward and greeted him. "Don't worry about it. I'm Ephemer!"

Everyone else took that opportunity to introduce themselves as well.

The fifth arrival placed a respectful hand against his own chest and bowed. "I apologize for making you wait. I was searching for something, and time got away from me. My name is Lauriam. It's nice to meet you all."

With that, the five Union leaders were assembled.

You were dreaming again.

"Ephemer... Skuld...," you moaned, tossing and turning.

I lay atop your chest, having the same dream as you.

Right now, you were taking a nap in a forest. Around you, birds were singing, and fluffy dandelion seeds floated through the air...

Eventually, your eyes cracked open, and you gave me a pat on the head to wake me up.

"That same dream again?"

"A dream..."

You slowly pushed yourself up and shook your head.

"Ever since that day, you've seen it so many times. Are you all right?"

"What day?" you asked dubiously.

That day.

"Master Ava asked you to join the Dandelions, and you talked

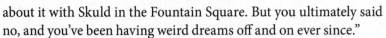

about it with Skuld in the Fountain Square. But you ultimately said no, and you've been having weird dreams off and on ever since."

You didn't seem convinced.

"Well, you've had a rough time of it lately; you're probably just worn out. It's a new world, so you should feel free. Why not take it easy once in a while?"

My suggestion didn't seem to sit well with you, though. I started to walk off on my own; we had to hurry through the forest, and it would be for the best if you forgot about that dream.

You followed after me.

Once we made our way out of the woods, we found large briar patch with an enormous castle visible beyond it.

This world was called the Enchanted Dominion.

"Guess we won't be going this way. How about we call it a day for now and come back when we've found another way through?"

You agreed with my idea.

Above, a single raven flew overhead.

"If only we had wings, too. Anyway, let's head home."

With that, we returned to Daybreak Town.

—Right around then, in front of the castle surrounded by thorny vines, the raven landed on the shoulder of a black-robed woman clutching a staff.

"Excellent," she murmured, and the bird gave a little *quork* in response. The woman—Maleficent—surveyed the area. "Still, I wonder where he's gone this time."

With a swirl of her robe, Maleficent began to walk toward the castle.

"No matter. Sora and the rest of those fools are powerless here. They cannot hinder us now."

She cackled as she always did—as she had in another time—and vanished.

*   *   *

Back Daybreak Town, on the hill overlooking its streets, I was speaking to Ephemer and Skuld.

"I see, so he is having dreams…," Skuld said sadly.

"Uh-huh. It's hard seeing him like that, and I hate lying… But I know it's for the best."

My gaze drifted toward my feet. You were better off without those memories, I was sure of it. Skuld patted me on the head. "It is. And it might be hard, but you're doing a great job."

"Of course! We're best friends."

"I can tell," she smiled.

"Chirithy, don't forget about your task," said Ephemer.

"I won't! Union Cross, right?" They had told me about this earlier.

"That's right. New adventures with friends is a great way to bury sad memories deep within one's heart," Skuld said earnestly, as if saying the words aloud could make them come true.

Then, Ephemer said something surprising. "The darkness in this world is not the same as what we faced in the other one."

A different darkness? But this world was still so new.

"It feels more…complex, like there's more to it than meets the eye. Almost like it has its own will."

Ephemer was sensitive to these things, so hearing this from him made me nervous.

What did he mean by "its own will"?

"Don't worry, we'll look into it. In the meantime, you know what your job is. Fill him in on everything, okay?" Skuld stated gently.

I nodded. "Will do!"

Then, I started making my way back to you.

*   *   *

Once they were alone, Ephemer and Skuld continued the conversation.

"What was that about? There's no need to worry anyone until we know for sure what it is."

Skuld thought it was careless of Ephemer to mention this mysterious "will." It was too heavy a burden for Chirithy to bear now.

"I know. I'm sorry, but this concerns everyone. I get a really bad feeling every time something happens in this world that didn't happen in the other one. This Union Cross business also feels...off. Something's not right."

They would have to do battle with those tainted by evil and darkness once more if they were going to take back the light.

"But we were told to make it happen. It's in the rules, remember?"

Leading the Unions and the world that had been placed under their care, there were rules that had to be followed. Going against them was not an option.

Ephemer crossed his arms. "I know, but... 'May your heart be your guiding key.'"

May your heart be your guiding key—